Operation Deep Dive

A Step into the Past

Author:
Dr. Terry Oroszi

Greylander Press

Operation Deep Dive:
A Step into the Past

ISBN:978-0-9821683-7-0

I dedicate this book to the people of Tres Piedras, New Mexico because I have used their village is represented as the home base for Eve and her family. The village of Tres Piedras exists, and the places mentioned are on the map, but the village residents and their philosophy are works of fiction.

Table of Contents

v

Chapter One

So It Begins

Eve was confronted by the intense sunlight the minute she opened the front door and walked out. Momentary blindness caused her to stumble. The positioning of a nearby column was the only thing that prevented her fall. She paused to recover; her eyes narrowed to a slit. *Walking in one's yard should not be so dangerous.* On the upside, the stroll to the mailbox was Eve's chance to breathe without her children at her side.

The hike to the mailbox was short, so she hadn't bothered to grab her sunglasses, a staple for every good

FBI agent.

The morning smelled of fresh-cut grass, fragrant flowers, and newly paved roads. The day would be beautiful and sunny, but in Alabama, almost every day is a beautiful, sunny, humdrum, boring kind of bloody day.

She looked about with satisfaction at the artificial order surrounding her. Seven nearly identical cookie-cutter homes lined the road, with manicured lawns, clean sidewalks, dedicated flower gardens, and each home complimenting the next. The community may have been new, but it was designed to look like old-money plantation homes.

Her house sat on a quiet suburban cul-de-sac, in the heart of Cottage Hill, near Mobile. You did not find this kind of living in New York City. Real estate properties were much lower in Alabama, affording them the ability to purchase a home for the same monthly costs as her rental back in Brooklyn. Boy, did she miss that place.

She no longer experienced the money struggles that shaped her youth; her husband's mother came from a wealthy family, and her love came in the form of material items. It brought her mother-in-law pleasure to shower them with gifts of money, vehicles, anything they wanted or needed. Yet, even with the beauty and order all around, Eve could not recall a time in her life feeling so completely underwhelmed.

She walked with great care, avoiding the cracks in the pavement. God knows why. Probably haunts from her childhood, when she was afraid that if she stepped on one, she would hurt her mother's back, and her mother would be unable to return to Eve and her father. There were not a lot of sidewalks or cracks in the deserts, and Eve avoided them all, but her mother never returned to them. Yes, stupid superstitions, but she continued to step carefully until she reached the mailbox.

It's strange that something as simple as a trip to the mailbox was such an important part of her day. Her actions were subtle, but an observant eye would notice the extra pep in each step. Eve was positively eager as she readied herself to open the black box, a door to the unknown. She was about to have contact with the outside world, with someone other than her husband, the nanny, her newborn, and the mini-Eve toddler running about inside.

As expected, there was a stack of mail, different colors, sizes, and weights. A quick flip-through indicated that at least half of them were junk, the others, likely bills. All of it required a more thorough investigation.

Eve was in the last month of her three-month maternity leave, and she was stir crazy. Going through the mail piece by piece gave her something to do that didn't involve diapers or baby sharks.

She made it back to the two-story colonial and slipped off her shoes just in time to hear her two-year-old daughter tiptoeing down the open-tread staircase. Harper was supported only by the spindles because, at under three-foot-tall, she was too short to reach the handrail. Nevertheless, she had mastered going up the stairs this way much sooner than going down them. Harper was sporting her favorite superman pajamas, and jumped off the bottom step, pretending to fly. Eve could not help but smile. She remembered those days when she too had a vivid imagination, and believed being a superhero was possible.

Her husband, Franklin, was the decorator in the family and the home reflected his taste. All his talk during their first date about not enjoying growing up in England in his parents' drafty estate home was clearly a lie. Everything in the home screamed British colonialism.

Teak woods, textiles printed with exotic patterns depicting local scenes, flora, and fauna, and beautifully aged, well-traveled chocolate and tan leather trunks with tarnished brass buckles and clasps. Eve didn't mind; she liked the style. It evoked a bygone era that was genteel and elegant while at the same time appearing relaxed and comfortable, so different from the sand-ridden trailers and tents from her youth.

The same theme was carried into the nursery. Replacing the deep mahogany and brown finishes found in the rest of the home. This room, dedicated to children and play, sported fresh whites and soft grays with whitewashed hardwood floors, ceiling fans, and, in place of curtains or blinds, plantation shutters. The room boasted a rattan rocking chair, a simple canopy bed with make-shift rails for Harper, and a white teak crib for Franklin.

The floors were littered with plush rugs, colorful, oversized pillows, and stuffed exotic animals of all sizes. A crayon-decorated white bookcase was home to books, puzzles, and board games. Trunks were chock-full of toys. Harper's doll house and baby doll kitchen were kept well-ordered and off the floor. Eve accepted no excuses for it to be otherwise. Harper was still transitioning into a big-girl bed, so she had access to her playthings throughout the night. On more than one occasion, Eve woke in the early morning hours to hear her daughter singing as she played happily by herself in the nursery.

Eve had no idea kids could be so messy, but a maid showed up every day after breakfast and tidied up the place, making life more tolerable. She ordered the house and was gone before Eve returned from the gym. Back at the Society for Humanity (SFH) commune where she grew up, there were very few young people, and cleanliness seemed to be a priority for all the residents. Sure, one or two people were just a little "unique" in their attire and space, but they were the exceptions.

Eve opened the fridge and pulled out a pitcher of unsweetened organic apple juice, and filled a sippy cup for Harper. She had to give it a taste. The name sounded awful. *What kind of person drinks unsweetened juice?* Her first impulse was to spit it out into the sink, but she managed to swallow. It truly was unpleasant and she couldn't believe her daughter drank the stuff.

After distracting Harper with a video and food, Eve sat down at the table, ready to sort through the mail. The amount of paper waste annoyed Eve. *Do people not understand it's the electronic age?* The stack was high, so she categorized the pile into junk, bills, and other. She found one of particular interest. It was a 5 x 7 Manila envelope with a disk and string closure and no return address. How fascinating.

Eve opened it carefully because she feared paper cuts, not out of worry that she might damage the contents. Paper cuts were the absolute worst. Eve was sure that she would rather take a bullet than have a paper cut, *but,* she supposed, *it depended on where the shot enters the body.* Eve admonished herself for being so easily sidetracked. She stared back down at the envelope with anticipation.

What she pulled out was a series of photos of herself from three years prior. Not just any photos, but ones that made her heart skip a beat. Eve, as a rule, tried, albeit largely unsuccessfully, to control her emotions. And when alone in her kitchen, looking at photos that could likely change her life, her emotions ran wild.

The tingling started at her toes and spread throughout her body. Her mind was racing, and her heart was thumping so loud she was sure everyone in the house could hear it. Eve dropped the packet and pictures back onto the table, got up abruptly, and moved to the counter to make herself a cup of *Death Wish* coffee.

The high caffeine content, and the fact that it was made in upstate New York, were just two of the reasons this brand was her favorite. Unlike her go-to, *Starbucks,* it was smooth and easy to drink. She was thankful those dreaded nine months of pregnancy were over.

Eve paused, one elbow on the counter, eyes wide, she stared at the items on the table, while listening to the water from the *Keurig's* resevour gurgle down into the machine, and eventually make its way through the coffee grounds and into her cup. Eve returned to the chair, took a deep swallow, enjoying the coffee's cherry and chocolate notes, and sat back down. A smile cracked her face. Oh boy, did she have a good feeling about this day.

Eve picked up the photos, one at a time. The images were clear, very professional, definitely not a product of CCTV. God knows she's seen her share of the grainy quality CCTV snaps. *Why, in this day and age, can they not improve the quality?* She knew the answer, CCTV captures everyone in the frame, equally, whereas a camera has a focus. Unlike Eve at the moment. When did she become so easily distracted, this would have never happened when she was working in the field.

In one shot she could make out her own face, under a black, curly wig, on the street outside the hotel. In another, she was easily recognizable, holding the gun used to shoot two security officers. A third photo was a picture of Eve with the backpack containing the bomb that would cause the destruction of an insurance company on Wall Street. But then, there were more, all showing Eve on that eventful day three years earlier. It seemed like a lifetime ago.

At the time of the bombing, Eve had been an active FBI agent, fresh off an undercover assignment. Still, the activities in the photos were not sanctioned by the FBI, because as we all know, the FBI does not sanction killing, ever.

The images documented Eve's part in a plot she and her father had carried out in homage to her stepmother and as a warning to insurance agencies," Change your ways, or you'll be next." In other words, based on the definition of terrorism, Eve and her father were domestic terrorists. However, this behavior was a one-time thing, not a career path.

Three years ago, Special Agent Evelyn "Eve" Black was part of the New York FBI field office and worked a particular case going undercover at the International Defense Exhibition Conference (IDEC). Unbeknownst to her boss, Special Agent in Charge (SAC) Adam Lange, Eve had another motive, she needed to find a terrorist cell to blame for the planned bombing.

The insurance company canceled Camilla's coverage when she was diagnosed with Diabetes Mellitus Type 2. Insulin costs were so high that she was forced to parcel out what little medicine she could afford. After a few weeks of inadequate self-regulation, she fell into a diabetic coma and never recovered.

John, Eve's father, was oblivious to Camilla's plight and her death shocked him. There were several reasons he could blame himself: such as never bothering to get a real job, with better insurance. Instead, he had relied on his online hacking business to provide for his family. In John's eyes, the fault was not his. He blamed a flawed government, one that did not care about the poor and disenfranchised. The government gave too much power to insurance companies, and the American people suffered.

Eve's childhood had been unique. Her father, Leonard Wilkins, AKA John Black, was a member of the socialist college group, turned terrorist organization, the Weatherman. When the Weatherman was deemed a terrorist group, her father, mother, and young Eve went underground to prevent the FBI from finding and arresting Leonard as one of the outspoken leaders of the faction.

Eve spent her first years continually on the move with her parents, rarely spending more than a night or two in any one location. The nomadic lifestyle was too much for Eve's mother. She was unable to cope, so she left her small family and moved back to Michigan with her parents. John survived his wife's departure thanks to the support of his Weatherman friends.

When Eve was five years old, John and several of his socialist comrades caravaned to New Mexico, thirty miles north of Taos, and started a commune. The population grew over time, and the community evolved into the village of Tres Piedras, New Mexico.

The community continued to foster an atmosphere of anti-government intellectuals and became a home for anyone with similar beliefs. Because of his role with the Weatherman, John was the unofficial leader of the leaderless settlement. Even some thirty years later, the flock looked to him for guidance and advice.

When Eve's mother left her husband and small daughter, John was crushed. He spiraled into depression. Drinking heavily and isolating himself, he left raising his daughter to the community. Several years later, when Eve was a spunky, adventurous, and somewhat ill-mannered ten-year-old, Camilla visited the compound.

She met and fell in love with both John and his young daughter, and never left. Camilla changed their lives. John put aside his drinking and rejoined the small society, and little Eve had a mother again. Camilla brought love and structure to her new family and the group.

Life in the desert was isolated and quiet. As a community, the residents chose not to be distracted by television, the government's tool to spread its message to the masses. Instead they listened to music, read books and had lengthy socialist-leaning discussions, and invited the few children to engage. Eve's father was the exception. There was an old military bunker on the land, one of the primary reasons in which they squatted there so many years ago.

Inside that bunker he had a short wave radio, the only way he had at the time to relay telephone and telegraph communications over great distances. The obsession to be connected, evolved from short waves into wifi. Computers occupied much of her father's time in her early years. Eve had very few friends and spent much of her time alone.

Keenly observant and aware of her and the community's uniqueness, she watched and listened to people in the stores and on the streets during supply runs in the nearby town. Eve learned to imitate the behavior of others very well, reading their body language, observing both verbal and nonverbal methods of communication, and mimicking their mannerisms. This was a skill she perfected over the years.

When Eve left her home in New Mexico for Columbia University in New York, her childhood upbringing in the small desert community made her an ill-fit among her wealthy, highly socialized classmates. Social interaction was not the only thing that left her feeling like an outcast; everything made her feel this way, right down to the television shows and movies her contemporaries often referenced. The first semester at the university was difficult. Still, she could blend in using the talent that she had been honing since age twelve.

Her keen sense of observation and her ability to adapt, chameleon-like, made her an excellent candidate for the FBI. Unfortunately, her career choice was not popular with her father or the community back home. She became a Tres Piedras pariah.

Eve's only communication with her childhood home came in the form of late-night phone conversations with her stepmother. Their bond continued to evolve until that fateful day when Eve received a call from her father saying Camilla was in the hospital. After nearly ten years, she returned home to bury her beloved stepmother and reconnect with her father and the Tres Piedras community.

United by grief after Camilla's death, Eve and her father could forgive each other for the years of estrangement. Eve feared that her father would drown his sorrow in liquor and become a recluse like the time after her mother left. Instead, they spent hours in a heated conversation about the government's failures and the power of the insurance monopolies.

For the first time, Eve understood the passion that inspired her father to join the Weatherman Underground. She wanted to keep her father busy, to prevent another downward spiral. They needed to teach a lesson to the insurance company that dropped Camilla. Eve stepped away from the FBI's "everything-is-black-and-white" mindset and entered a gray zone. Together with her father, they devised a plan to take down the insurance company in Camilla's honor.

Destroying the Pacific Mutual Insurance (PCI) company was no small feat. John, an engineer, turned computer hacker, designed a virus constructor or VC, a malicious program that could create new viruses with an interface that allows it to choose the characteristics of the created malware. With this VC, he could wipe the PCI's computers, their servers, and online backup storage. Meanwhile, Eve had planted a bomb on the first floor of the company's headquarters, removing the building from the Wall Street landscape. Unfortunately, she had to shoot and fatally wound two security officers in the process. The photos she now held in her hand recalled those events with glaring incrimination.

Eve sat at the kitchen table on her perfectly manicured street, sipping her just-right, strong, black coffee, and pondered the prints displayed in front of her. Finally, a decision had to be made: she could disrupt her perfect little life, track down the photographer, or ignore the photos, and continue her life with her perfect little family in her perfect little house and her perfect little FBI desk job.

Eve was living the American dream, and at this moment, with that dream in jeopardy, Eve could not have been happier. Spending one more day in this charade of life was enough to drive her insane. She knew what she had to do. In no time her phone was out and she was speaking to her father.

John's life had changed quite a bit since the death

of his Camilla. Thanks to Eve and her friendship with Nadia Katz, an Israeli weapons trainer, and spy, he had a beautiful young girlfriend. John also served as a surrogate grandfather for two preteen girls Eve and Nadia had rescued from the Hutaree Michigan militia group. He answered the phone on the first ring, "Hello Evie," reverting to her childhood nickname.

"Dad, we have a problem." Eve went on to tell him about the photos and what would happen if they were seen by anyone, ever!

Her father's advice was simple, "Figure out who took the photos and take them out before anyone finds out what we did."

She was glad he was on the phone instead of face-to-face, so he couldn't see her eye roll. She didn't need her dad to tell her this.

John sighed, signaling that, although he didn't see the eye roll, he certainly knew it happened, "Evie, bring the kids to Tres Piedras; we'll work this out together."

Eve immediately felt both relieved and excited. When her father said he could fix something, she knew he could, and she felt somewhat like a child with a large present in front of her, waiting to be opened. She was grinning ear to ear and already making travel plans in her head when she hung up the phone.

The final step was to tell Franklin that a vacation to Tres Piedras was forthcoming. Easy... the new baby needs to meet his grandpa.

Eve met her husband, Franklin, when he and his FBI team of computer experts, the Dream Team, were creating her undercover persona for the IDEC. With the team's help, she became the terrorism researcher and author, Dr. Nicole Mathers.

Unfortunately for Eve, the IDEC mission debriefing did not go as planned. Her SAC had pointed out her deficient undercover skills and recommended anger management classes. But, seriously, what did he know? *Okay, so maybe she dropped cover once or twice during the conference and maybe a few people lost their lives because of her temper, but who doesn't get a little emotional when dealing with complex individuals?* Eve seriously doubted he even knew about the unsanctioned dead people.

The anger management classes may have been a good idea: the meditation techniques that she learned still occasionally found their way into Eve's morning routine, right after coffee, but before real clothes, unless she was experiencing one of those yoga-pants-loose-shirt kinds of days. Eve noticed her stress level plummet and her good mood spike on those days. Whether that was caused by the coffee or the spandex, she didn't want to know.

Coffee was Eve's go-to when she felt happy, sad, annoyed, anxious..., *okay, anytime.* After that illuminating debrief with her SAC three years ago, she headed straight to *Starbucks*, not the one at 111 Worth St. That one may have been only a minute walk from the FBI building. The floor plan was too open. The wood shelves stacked with coffee accessories on the outside walls and the communal tables were definitely not Eve's style.

14

Back then, she preferred the *Starbucks* on Broadway, which was only a three-minute walk. That one had all the nooks and crannies necessary for isolation from the world. Eve missed New York. The *Starbucks* closest to her home in Mobile, Alabama, was eight to twelve miles away. She had the option of three different routes involving two different interstates. However, it still took twenty minutes to get there. This was just one of the many reasons she hated Alabama.

Franklin was at the *Starbucks* on Broadway when Eve slumped in, feeling dejected after the debrief. He was surrounded by papers, his computer, and enjoying a beverage. She accepted the seat he offered. During the IDEC conference, they had some back-and-forth banter that was akin to a boy pulling the girls' pigtails; in other words, he liked her. The two went from coffee to beer to bed, and just weeks later, he proposed.

This was the second time someone had proposed marriage to Eve. Back at Quantico, when she was training to become an agent, she dated an FBI Analyst trainee. During the first twelve weeks of instruction, the agents and analysts worked and trained together, but then the analysts were sent to their first duty station while the agents continued at Quantico.

The analyst boyfriend had arranged an elaborate hike in the woods that opened up onto a secluded sandy beach on the Potomac River. Aaron had a picnic basket, and an old plaid blanket already prepared. He had planned to propose there, and she knew it. It the scene was perfectly cliché, and off-putting to Eve. The look of disgust written across her face was undeniable. Aaron realized it and reacted poorly. He called her a few names that she would rather not remember, walked away, and Eve never saw him again.

Fortunately, that same look was not as noticeable when Franklin asked her to marry him. Eve was better skilled at hiding her emotions this time around. She said yes, because that was what she was supposed to do. Eve was adept at mimicking positive societal behaviors. At her age and in her career, she could only benefit from being married to Franklin, the son of an American diplomat, and a well-respected professional in the FBI community. So, of course, she said yes.

Immediately following their marriage, two things happened that changed her life. They were transferred to Mobile, Alabama, and Eve found out she was expecting their first child. Becoming a mother was something Eve had never wanted, but she decided to go through with it in honor of her stepmother's Catholic beliefs and to make her father a grandpa, something Eve knew he wanted.

Regrettably, what this meant for Eve was that she was no longer out in the field taking down bad guys. Instead, she was stuck in an office, doing paperwork and, in her words, "Getting fat."

After their daughter, Harper, was born, she had to wait three months to go back to work, and those months could not have ended soon enough. After just eight weeks back on the job and doing all she could to lose the weight she had gained, Eve was pregnant again.

This time she gave birth to a little boy, Franklin Jefferson Johnson IV. The name was not her choice, *seriously, who wants to have three US presidents' names?* Eve proved that she appreciated big names for little things when she named her puppy, Sebastian, so why not a little baby? She conceded.

After their second child, Eve gave Franklin three choices: number one, get a vasectomy; number two, no more sex; or three, she would take a goddamn knife and cut it off. He chose the vasectomy, *wise man.*

The only way Eve could cope with motherhood was to employ a nanny. The daily routine of raising children left her feeling out of control, something she could not tolerate. Every morning when Harper woke, she was in a terrible mood, creating chaos in the house.

Franklin blamed their daughter's behavior on Eve, saying something about his wife's pre-coffee mood. Eve pretended to have no idea what he was talking about, but, okay, maybe Harper did get most of her attitude from her mom, but that didn't reduce the stress she felt when the child was around. It did make her wonder how Franklin could handle both of them with such ease. *Maybe that was why he left the house so early every day?*

When Eve made breakfast for her petulant toddler, all the little girl did was complain about how long the toast took to pop up, the funny tasting butter, the lack of PB&J, or how the eggs were not just right. Her tantrums were a daily problem, but Harper did settle down once she had something to eat.

Before her son was born, when Eve was able to go to work every morning, her daughter became annoyingly clingy, and wanted her mommy to play. She cried big crocodile tears and clung when she sensed she was not the center of her mommy's world, and then followed her around until satisfied with the amount of attention she received. The bad behavior returned once Franklin Jefferson Johnson IV came home from the hospital.

Eve was proud of her daughter. Harper was very verbal and talked in full, complex sentences. She loved books and would sit and listen to Eve read to her for as long as Eve could endure. Harper had a great sense of humor and was friendly with other kids. Some days were great, and she would be very calm, especially if she had gotten plenty of sleep. Then, there were the other days, the ones where she started throwing 30-second tantrums with a shrill whine that made Eve feel like she would lose her mind. Had it been anyone else's child, Eve wouldn't have borne it as well.

Eve hired Sharlo, an intelligent dark-haired girl with a beautiful smile from Tres Piedras, to move in and help care for the children. Living near Mobile meant Sharlo could attend the local college and experience life outside that tight-knit, rural, Tres Piedras group. They chose Sharlo because of her kind, caring, and peaceful personality, quite the opposite of Eve, but also because she was a martial arts devotee and would be able to protect the children. Sharlo also doubled as a sparring partner for Eve.

Their home had an attached conservatory, designed to be used as a sun room or greenhouse. However, Eve had other ideas for the space. She converted it into a gym and used it when she didn't want to use the equipment at the FBI's fitness center, or when leaving home and being around people proved to be too much for her.

The concept of being a people-person was foreign to Eve. She could not conceive of being comfortable with strangers, content with crowds. There was something about the shadows that soothed Eve. They were a haven for her, a place where her soul could be renewed. Her home gym retreat, with glass walls and ceiling, was the place to be when the children and Franklin were asleep.

With an unencumbered view of the stars above, Eve would take out her frustration on a punching bag, some free weights, or her yoga mat. She left the center of the room open so she and Sharlo could spar. This was an opportunity for Eve to improve her skills and help keep Sharlo's abilities on point. One never knew when a criminal may choose to go after the children of FBI parents.

Sharlo had learned from her parents the Japanese martial art of *Aikido*, a practice influenced by China and India that involves throwing, joint locking, striking, and pinning techniques, coupled with training in traditional Japanese weapons such as the sword, staff, and knife. It emphasizes the development of internal awareness, as well as physical prowess, and personal integrity, the ideal to fight only when needed, and with compassion and insight. The follower of *Aikido* is expected to be a model of uprightness, courage, and loyalty, willingly sacrificing life in the name of principle and duty. *Aikido* promotes positivity with a path to self-development.

Make no mistake, Eve loved her children as much as she could. The love she felt may not be the same as other mothers, she would never know, it's not like she could get inside their heads to know how her feelings compared to theirs. Nevertheless, Eve believed that they were hers to protect, and she would never let anything bad happen to them. Her responsibility was clear, give them as perfect a life as possible. That was how Eve demonstrated her love for the children, husband, and even for her extended family in Tres Piedras.

Eve spent every day, after the birth of her son, in the gym so she could get in shape. Eve needed to get back to work, chasing bad guys, the work that she was meant to do. Eve anticipated her return to the field much like a young person awaiting the start of summer vacation.

The mere existence of the photos, if they ever got out, would surely fuck up her life. She had to take care of this, or lose everything: her job, her lifestyle, her freedom, and her father. So that night, when Franklin arrived home, Eve gave him the news that she wanted to take her children to her father's for a visit.

Franklin lived a much-pampered life growing up outside London, England, in an oversized home on a well-maintained estate, with servants and boarding schools, and, as with upper-class Brits, there was an emotional and sometimes physical disconnect between children and parents. He barely batted an eye when Eve declared that she was taking his two-year-old daughter and his nearly two-month-old son for an extended vacation. Franklin adored his wife, she was more important to him than anything in the world, and he knew she was unhappy. His biggest fear was that he would lose her, so if taking a trip to New Mexico would make life better for her, he supported it without question.

Sharlo packed the children's things. She missed her parents, the desert, and the slow pace of Tres Piedras, and was thrilled to be going back home. In the village, her time was spent working with her parents, training the villagers of all ages in self-defense and martial arts, and learning to be a first responder in Carlson, a small town south of Tres Piedras. Her ultimate goal was to attend medical school and focus on community and tribal health care.

After spending a significant amount of time with Eve, in the home, and when training, Sharlo recognized the mother's lack of maternal instincts, and was pleased that Eve was self aware enough to reach out for help. She knew the family depended on her to be the nurturing force in their children's lives.

Eve was just as elated as Sharlo to be going to the land of sand, peace, and isolation. She had no idea what to pack, so she just packed everything she owned or everything that she could wear in public without embarrassment.

Early the following day, Franklin drove them the eight miles to the airport, leaving his family at the curb so he could drive the nearly twenty miles back to the FBI office.

There were plasma screens of arrival and departure times on the airport wall. In the background, soft classical music played, punctuated by the robotic voice reminding passengers not to lose sight of their personal possessions. Sharlo held the baby, her carry-on, the diaper bag, and luggage.

Eve had Harper sitting on her suitcase, the girl's legs dangling while holding onto the suitcase's extended handle. She maneuvered it through the noisy crowd straight up to the ticket counter. Harper's laughter throughout the ride was infectious. Nearly everyone they passed smiled at the little girl and barely noticed the mother. This was just as well because the look on Eve's face, the hard smile, the tense muscles, and the dismissive air would have ruined the happy moment they were experiencing.

People were lined up at the check-in desk with their suitcases and baggage. Eve bypassed them all and walked up to the counter. With a don't-mess-with-me look on her face, she flashed her FBI credentials, handed over the forms required by the airlines when an agent is carrying a firearm, and informed the lady behind the counter, in her typical curt manner, that she was armed. The counter attendant asked to see the weapon.

Eve raised an eyebrow and gave her a glassy stare, "The last thing I will do is pull out a handgun in front of all these people in the ticket line. Please call your supervisor over."

The attendant quickly changed her mind, and returned Eve's things, including the necessary special boarding passes.

Eve knew the protocol: the pilot would be advised that Eve was there, with a weapon, and in seat 17C. The polite thing to do would be to ask to meet the captain, and notify the head flight attendant of her status and ask if anyone else was traveling armed on the flight. If so, have them identified and go up and introduce herself to them. That was not happening. Eve did not want to meet anyone, not the captain, the flight attendants, nor any of the passengers on the plane, carrying or not.

They made it to the gate with plenty of time to spare. Eve left the children with Sharlo and picked up some snacks over at *Hudson News,* and then a robust dark coffee for her, and a green tea for Sharlo at *Carpe Diem Coffee and Tea.* With full hands, she then returned to wait the thirty-eight minutes to board. Finding seats open for three next to each other was impossible.

Eve sat a few rows away from Sharlo and the children. She kept the jellybeans for herself and surrendered the rest of the goodies to Sharlo and Harper. Now they just had to wait for the plane to arrive, the passengers to disembark, and then it would be their time to board.

Eve was prepared to wait patiently for the plane, but even the best intentions can be foiled. As soon as a travelers left their seats next to her, two male teens wearing baggy pants, exposed boxers, carrying oversized backpacks, sat down on either side of her. She had purposely picked this spot so no one would be near her, yet here they were, self absorbed, loud-mouthed young punks, and did not recognize Eve's mood rapidly changing as they continued to talk across her to each other.

Finally, she just had to say it: "Listen, boys, you'll have to move, FBI business."

"Oh lady, who you think you fooling, you ain't no goddamn FBI and YOU need to move." The two punks started laughing as if they had just cracked a great joke.

Eve turned to the one that suggested she move. She opened her jacket with one hand, revealing her piece, and pulled out her badge with the other, then tucked both away and said in a voice that dared anyone to challenge, "Listen to me, you little punk, you'll get the hell away from me this very minute, or I am going to make sure you're never able to fly on a plane again. You hear me?"The two moved away so fast that Eve wondered why she had waited so long to threaten them. *Ahhh...peace.* She glanced over at Sharlo and the children. Sharlo was looking at her and did not look pleased. Busted. Eve was the grown-up here. Why did this young woman make her feel dressed down like she was a child? Eve knew Sharlo was blessed with the morals and kindness of an angel, which was why she had the power. But, at times like this, Eve hated it.

An elderly lady was the next one to invade her space. Eve had a rule for older people and children: she would go out of her way to help people that fell into those two demographics. Eve showed the woman her badge and asked her if she needed anything. There is typically a degree of implied trust when a badge is shown to strangers. The woman said she was awfully thirsty, so Eve went back to *Hudson News* and got her water. When she returned, an older man was in her seat and a young lady in the other one.

She handed the older lady the bottled water, and the lady said, "Meet my husband and daughter; we're flying to New Mexico."

Eve couldn't help but feel like the old woman had just played her, to take the once-occupied seat. Bravo to her. When she glanced over at Sharlo and saw her smile, Eve knew she had just made up for the previous incident with the two boys. Eve decided to stand. The wait couldn't be more than five or ten minutes.

Once settled, leaning on a wall near the gate counter, she took a sip of her forgotten coffee, long since devoid of warmth, and shuddered, spilling some on her shirt. Eve wasn't sure if she had time to find a bathroom and wash it, but she would hurry. The queue at the ladies' room was out the door. She passed the people in line and announced while going in, "I just need the sink."

Someone in the line said, "Yeah, I bet."

Eve turned to look daggers at the woman. She was in her mid-60s with long gray flowing locks and perfect brilliant white teeth. The kind of woman who has made several visits to her plastic surgeon's office. *You know the type.*

Eve set her coffee down, grabbed a paper towel, dabbed some soap, and had it cleaned, or nearly so, in no time. She looked in the mirror and saw the mouthy lady behind her. Eve twirled around so that her carry-on bag was swinging, and her cold coffee spilled out and onto the lady's silk white blouse and gray pants. "Oh ma'am, I'm so sorry." Which would have been believable had she not snickered at the end. Eve didn't care. Sharlo was nowhere around, and she made it back to the gate in time to board without waiting.

Chapter Two

Back in Tres Piedras

She was now one of them, a mother on a plane with a crying baby and another child busy kicking the seat in front of her. Sharlo had the window seat and Eve the aisle. Harper sat between them, and the two took turns with Franklin. The baby was not compatible with the name. In fact, Eve could not imagine any baby fitting the name Franklin, except for maybe her husband. His name was never shortened to Frank or Frankie.

A balding middle-aged gentleman wearing what appeared to be an ill-fitting, oversized suit and tie was sitting in 16B, the middle seat in the aisle in front of Harper. The man would sigh, in a loud and exaggerated fashion, with an occasional turnaround to glare at Harper and Eve whenever her daughter kicked his seat or when baby Franklin made too much noise.

In most circumstances, Sharlo's presence would bring to the space a calmness. She could inject a little peace into a potentially explosive environment, but she was of little help today. Her reasons were valid, she was exhausted from the children and excited to be going home, but in actuality, this man got on her nerves.

Sharlo would play a game to help Eve with her anger management issues when the situation required. They often did this when in crowded conditions that were often stressful for Eve. Together they would make up reasons to explain why a person of interest was in such a bad mood. The grounds had to make sense in the context of the environment, so in this case the man in question was on the plane, between two passengers, wearing a suit too big for him, and was losing his hair. The game was an empathy tool that Sharlo learned in Aikido class.

She started, "He had weight-loss surgery and hasn't been able to eat ice cream in months."

Eve knew what Sharlo was doing and had trouble getting into the mood, but she tried, "His wife just divorced him for being too ugly."

Sharlo's next reason was spot on, "His briefs are riding up, and the seatbelt prevents him from fixing them."

Eve snickered at that one, and had one of her own, "He needs to pass gas and cannot do so without the surrounding people being affected."

With this one, the two women laughed so hard that even Harper started laughing. This caused the man, unaware that he was the source of their amusement, to turn around again and glare, amplifying the laughter.

Her game worked; Eve felt much better for about ten minutes until he started again.

Eve closed her eyes, took deep cleansing breaths, and attempted to meditate her anger away by plotting revenge scenarios. When the man got up to go to the lavatory, she could mess with his seat belt so it wouldn't latch, requiring him to sit elsewhere, but she couldn't do this without being noticed. Or, a smile spreading on her face, she could tamper with the lock on the lavatory door so he could not get out. No, this would also not work; she would get caught.

Doing either of those things would likely mean Eve would be having a conversation with the air marshal or the security people at the airport. She finally came up with a scenario that could be successful and, if done correctly, Eve wouldn't be blamed. When he walked down the aisle, she could put out her foot and trip him; maybe he would break his nose on a seat or sprain something. She nodded her head with satisfaction, and her smile turned just a little evil. That would work; accidents like that happen all the time. Now, how to get him up to use the bathroom.

Eve tapped him on the shoulder, "Excuse me, sir, I've noticed my children bothering you and would like to get you a beverage to show my appreciation of your tolerance, perhaps a tall glass of something cold? A Bloody Mary?"

He grunted a barely audible, "Yes, sure." When the flight attendant came around, Eve ordered the man a tall water and a Bloody Mary, double vodka. As soon as that one was finished, she ordered him another. Twenty minutes before landing, he started to get up from his middle seat, disrupting both the people to his left and right. When he made it to her aisle, she crossed her left leg over her right, just enough to cause him to stumble, and down he went.

As if choreographed, he hit the arm of the seat behind hers with his face. Blood started pouring out of his nose. She feigned shock and yelled out for the flight attendant, pulling off the concerned passenger well, with Sharlo being the only one in on her little game. For the rest of the trip, the bald man was moved to the back of the plane, his face covered with ice and towels. Eve heard the passengers mentioning with disgust his excessive alcohol consumption. She lay back in her seat and smiled.

The meditation worked very well this time. She would have to practice it more often when aggravated by others. Eve refused to look over at Sharlo. She knew the young woman would be giving her a look of disapproval for her method of handling the situation. Eve didn't care. She was feeling oddly satisfied.

They landed at the familiar Taos airport, rented a Jeep, and drove the thirty miles to the village. In the past, Eve usually made this trip alone, but not this time. She shook her head, thought about being alone in the desert, and drove faster. Finally, they made it to Tres Piedras alive and well. Eve dropped Sharlo off at her parent's straw-bale/post and beam off-grid home three miles off the highway across the Rio Grande Gorge Bridge.

Harper tried her best to get out of her car seat to go with HER Sharlo. When that proved unsuccessful, she screamed at the top of her lungs, with Franklin joining in. This continued the rest of the way to Eve's father's home, across from the railroad water tower.

They were met at the door by Mari, the mother of John's surrogate grandchildren. Mari, short for Marian, was a woman beholden to Eve and Nadia for rescuing her from a life of servitude and abuse with the Michigan Hutaree Militia. At the age of fourteen, Mari was given in exchange to the Hutaree Militia leader, Joshua Carter, by her father, an Ohio militiaman.

Eve had first met Joshua at the IDEC event when she was undercover as Dr. Mathers. Her first impression was that he reminded her of the Reverend Kane in the Poltergeist movie, both in personality and appearance. The last time Mari saw her mother, she was on the ground bleeding, after an unsuccessful attempt to stop her husband from sending their beautiful young daughter, with this creepy older man.

The rebellious behavior had earned her mother a fist to the face. Standing up to your husband when he is a member of the Ohio or Michigan militias would only result in abuse of some sort. Still, that circle is hard to break, and the women grew up knowing no other life.

They were kept at home, lacked formal education, and only dated and married men their fathers arranged or approved.

Mari had two daughters with her husband before she was sixteen and had suffered both physical and sexual abuse at the hands of her husband and his brothers. When Eve was at the IDEC, she endured Joshua Carter's braggadocio with disgust. She strategically enlisted the aid of a band of Aryan Nation members to kill him. Then, Nadia and Eve made a road trip to the Hutaree compound and rescued any female willing to leave. Mari was not passive in this rescue; Eve had given her a gun, and Mari shot and killed the Hutaree men that abused her. The women and children drove to Tres Piedras with Eve and Nadia and had been there.

As Eve stood at the open door of her father's home, Mari took the newborn boy into her arms and vowed never to let him go. She had an adoring look of maternal satisfaction on her face as she walked inside. Harper came up the stairs taking them one at a time until she made it onto the porch and stood up. She reached out to Eve to help steady herself as an enormous puppy came wiggling between Eve's legs, nearly knocking the toddler down.

John walked up to the door from his underground bunker behind the house, scooped up his granddaughter, and gave his daughter a peck on the cheek, "Welcome home, Evie."

Eve gave her father a quick once over, assessing his appearance and health. It had been nearly three years. But, she thought to herself, he looks great, younger.

After the explosion and the deaths of the security guards, John decided they should maintain a distance to keep others from putting two and two together. So other than her wedding to Franklin and the birth of her children, they had not seen one another. Harper did not remember her Papa, but she rarely knew a stranger and held onto him with one of her hands while exploring his facial stubble with the other. Harper never saw her daddy looking so rugged. He was always well-groomed and clean-shaven, so the stubble was strange to the two-year-old.

When rescued, Mari's daughters, Jada and Rose, were just young girls of twelve and ten. Had they stayed with the Hutaree group, they would have been given as wives to men more than twice their age for a life of submission, servitude, and abuse. The girls barely remembered those days. For the past three years, they had lived in Tres Piedras with their Papa John and Auntie Nadia, along with their mother. They attended school in the village and were surrounded by love. To the two teenagers, that love was overwhelming. Due to the infrequency of contact with Eve, they had developed a shyness around her and merely greeted her with a glance and a simple hello. Then they focused on their cell phones, giggling as they walked back to their rooms.

Once they agreed that the small family of three would be moving in permanently, the villagers helped John add an addition to his house. What was once a two-bedroom one-bath became a five-bedroom three-bath. Many villagers spent their days doing construction as a living, so work was done up to code and looked like it had been there for years. John's place was adobe style, typical for the area, and suitable for the hot, dry climate. The home's interior was spacious and clean, with aged, thick wood beams. A north view of the addition meant they could have big windows without heating up the place, so the rooms were bright with soft, indirect light.

His home was relatively smart. They could shut off the power with just the flick of a switch. Unique hiding spots existed, but only John knew about them. After an unexpected visit from an intrusive FBI agent, he installed cameras in the open spaces. Built-in speakers were strategically placed around the house because of John's love of music. Tonight, it seemed he was on a Rock Opera kick, a popular piece in the late 1960s. The style was inspired by composers like Tchaikovsky, Mussorgsky, and Berlioz. Rock Operas tell a story in a song format, utilizing the band's signature styles and wordplay to create a unique experience. David Bowie's Ziggy Stardust was the preference during dinner prep.

Mari knew food had the potential to help and heal others. This was her way of showing love and gratitude to her new family. Her cooking fed the soul, brought smiles and laughter, and made everything better. Mari reminded Eve of her dear Camilla, but only in her nurturing style. Camilla was born in Mexico, coming to the states at a very young age. She had café au lait skin and dark hair and eyes.

In contrast, Mari had pale skin, Nordic heritage, and was child-like in her proportions but clearly an adult. At the moment, she was pink in the face, with her blonde bangs pasted to her forehead with steam and sweat. Mari was dancing around as if she had her own personal opera playing within. There was a steady rhythm to her movements. It took just one peek into the kitchen to see how much she loved cooking.

Mari was preparing a German-style fried chicken, something she used to make in Michigan and one of her children's favorites. It did have a New Mexico twist because she had a variety of homemade salsas and a side of Nopales Frito (Fried Cactus). The teens appeared in the kitchen as if by magic and started setting the table for dinner. Eve was impressed and was ready to complement their sudden appearance and desire to help until she realized that Mari had texted them. Camilla would have had no problem raising her voice to get kitchen help from her family or even visiting neighbors back in the day.

The one person missing from the household was Nadia. She often disappeared for short periods because of her profession. No one questioned her movements, nor did anyone know what she did. Although, when they first met at the IDEC, Nadia had told Eve she was an Israeli weapons trainer, Eve was starting to suspect that was only part of her job. She was definitely a rock star with weapons. Her sense of style and sensuality made her more superhero than a housewife. What she was doing playing house with John and his family was still a mystery to them all.

Thanks to her profession, Eve learned to live by the Dragnet quote, 'Just the facts, ma'am,' so she found it quite natural to ask questions. This was not only born of her FBI life; it stemmed from her life in the village. They followed another motto, "If I need to know, you'll tell me." Living so close, practically on top of each other, meaning they had to create their own boundaries. This served people like the Black-Katz family, living lives based on professional secrets.

The mood of the house was celebratory, with many neighbors stopping by that evening to say hello and to be introduced to Harper and the new baby boy. But, unfortunately, the people and the energy were just a little too much for Eve, so when she finally had a chance to be alone with her father, she took it gratefully. They grabbed a couple beers and went outside.

The first thing out of his mouth was, "What did you tell Franklin?"

"I told him I was bringing the kids here to visit you. What else could I tell him? I have only three weeks of maternity leave left, then back to work. So hopefully, we can figure this out in under three weeks."

"It's wise you didn't tell him more. As I've told you before, there is just something about him that makes me uncomfortable, I don't like him."

"Oh, Dad, you don't like him because he was born privileged and works for the government. So he didn't have a chance of winning you over."

"I can't argue with you." He sipped his beer, "What you're saying is all true... but it's something else. It's like he's fake, flat, and predictable, like a character in a novel."

"He's fake? Tell me again, Dad, what's your name? Your real name."

John reached out and put his arm around Eve, "As long as he does right by you and my grandchildren, I will keep my mouth shut."

Eve changed the topic, "Well, Dad have you found out anything using your savvy Internet skills?"

"No luck; it looks like we'll have to do this the old fashioned way," he pulled out a notebook, tore off a piece of paper, grabbed a pen from his pocket and handed them to her, and said, "Write a list of people you interacted with prior to the explosion, and all your previous romantic relationships. Then, put an asterisk next to the ones that may have a reason not to like you. Once you've done with this, I'll start doing my own brand of background checks."

Eve sat down at the gray, weathered picnic table with pen and paper, ready to start. She appreciated the beautiful star-filled evening. Laughter and music filtered outside, and her dad was nearby. It wasn't until she was prepared to begin working on the list that she realized how difficult this would be.

Chapter Three

The Plan

Eve thought writing a list of the people that may be out to get her would be easy and short. In the past three years, she at least knew she would not have anyone to put on the list. Well, there was that lady in yoga class. She put her mat too close to Eve's mat, so Eve had to knock her down "accidentally." The poor thing sprained her wrist and could not return to class for several weeks.

Then there was the man at the grocery store standing with the door to the freezer foods wide open, his body in front of it, and his cart next to him, blocking the aisle.

Eve stood there, waiting an eternity for him to move himself or the cart; she didn't care which one. Finally, when he did not move, she walked up to his cart, gave it a very hard shove, and sent it down the aisle, right into the end display, knocking the cart and display over.

She should probably include Harper's babysitter, the young woman she hired before Sharlo came to live with them. Eve had returned to find the sitter and her boyfriend in the primary bedroom on the bed. She pulled her gun on the two of them, and the boyfriend was so frightened he urinated in his jeans while trying to pull them up.

The girl threatened to tell her mom, so Eve threatened to tell her mom, but it would be her version. Eve shared with the young couple how it would play out. She had arrived home and heard what was obviously a male voice, not her husband, and feared a home invasion. Obviously, Eve had a good reason to pull out her weapon and might even have shot him! After hearing Eve's version of the story, the two ran out of the house without Eve having a chance to pay the girl.

Now that she thought about it, her time in Alabama has been full of people who probably didn't like her and should be on the list; however, none of them would have known about the explosion or the security guards.

She decided she could break the list down into two columns, the people she met after joining the FBI and people before the FBI. Okay, now she was getting somewhere. Eve gulped down another swig of her beer and relaxed. People that may want to blackmail her, hmmmmm....

Just a few months before the explosion, Eve was undercover at the IDEC, and sure, a few of the people she encountered there may have had a problem with her, and one or two may have continued to observe her, without her knowing, but that's not likely, she's good at her job.

She started with the remaining members of the Hutaree Militia. The Aryan Nation guys had killed their leader, Joshua Carter, for "Dr. Mathers," and Mari had killed his brothers. Eve had killed one of the militia members during the rescue mission, but that left only a handful of men and a few women still alive. They would definitely want her dead, but she doubted they could find out who she really was. To the best of her knowledge, she had not broken cover in their presence.

The four Aryan Nation punks she met at the conference were a different story altogether. Eve found it highly unlikely that they had figured out how she set them up to do her dirty work. She didn't believe they had the skill, connections, or intellect to track her down. She also doubted they could have gotten those photos without her seeing them. They were part of a larger group living on a ten-acre compound in the town of Ulysses in north-central Pennsylvania. She didn't think they were responsible, but a road trip could be fun!

Then there was Rafael and his wife, Elaine. They were members of Jamaat al-Fuqura, an international Muslim terror organization. The two lived with several others on a compound in Charlotte County, Virginia. They weren't happy when they left the interview. Eve, as Dr. Mathers, had asked Rafael a tricky question, "Historically, the Jamaat al-Fuqura are known to commit firebombings and murders, do the al-Fuqura feel that the only way they can live peacefully is to promote violence?" The two stalked out with barely a goodbye.

The FBI paid each of the six groups she interviewed ten thousand dollars to answer her questions. By cutting the meeting short, Rafael risked not getting paid. She put their names on the list ahead of the Aryan Nation. The al-Fuqura did not have much money, and upsetting them may have made her a target. She thought back to the interview and how, in an attempt to connect with the couple, she carelessly told them about her father and revealed that she had grown up at the compound in New Mexico, thus making it easier for them to find out her true identity.

Another individual with whom she shared too much personal information was Campbell Greene, AKA "ELF man," a member of the Environmental Liberation Front. Eve loved nicknames and used them whenever possible. She had continued to email and text with ELF man over the years and knew he wanted more; however, it was best to keep him at a distance. Lately, his texts have taken on a different vibe. Maybe she should visit him as well.

She skipped over the America Ninja Muslim father and his sons, leaving them off the list. Their motivation was not like the others, and there was little chance they were involved. Eve shook her head, remembering she had broken cover with the dad and sons. While she did not condone killing Americans, she understood that the father was fighting overseas and sought revenge on behalf of someone that meant something special to him. How were her actions on Wall Street any different?

Eve had to pause. After recalling the interviews individually, she had to admit that she broke cover more than a few times. Several of the terrorists she interviewed at the conference knew a mix of Eve and her undercover persona, Dr. Nicole Mathers.

Dr. Mathers was a persona created by a team of FBI personnel. As Dr. Mathers, Eve became a terrorism researcher, academic, and author. In reality, the FBI hired two professors from UCLA and Berkeley to ghostwrite a book, The Mindset of a Terrorist, on her behalf. The FBI Dream team, led by her husband, had created an app called Bookbot. Names and variables of interest were inputted by humans. The program scanned the Internet, producing infographics and identifying patterns in the data. With the Bookbot app, they were able to create a second book, The American Terrorist.

The FBI team also paid pay-to-publish journals a little extra so they could have articles back-dated to demonstrate a long history of Dr. Mathers' publications in the field of terrorism. Finally, to shore up the persona, her FBI Dream team members invented a back-story for her, including creating fake social media accounts and thousands of fake followers.

They re-branded her as a fashion-conscious individual. They didn't want any recognizable trace of FBI Special Agent Eve. It would be Dr. Mathers reaching out to those she interviewed at the conference, but it would be Eve visiting any others that made it onto her list.

There was one terrorist cell that she was purposely

avoiding thinking about: the New York Four (NY4), Jackson, Bill, Jim, and Payton. The four were on the receiving end of Eve's strategic plan to shift blame for the terrorist act she and her father had planned and executed. After killing the security guards and detonating the bomb in the Pacific Mutual Insurance Company, Eve had placed a second bomb, identical to the first, in Jim's room. She also planted the gun that she used to kill the security guards in Bill's room.

She had meant for Jackson to go free. The only item she left in his room was a pair of borrowed sunglasses, but because of the glasses, Jackson was sure to know that Eve was involved.

Three of the NY4 were now in prison, Jackson, Bill, and Jim. Payton was acquitted, and she knew he was still living in New York with his wife and daughters. Jackson could have sent the photos to exact his revenge. Neither Payton nor Jackson should have been found guilty. Nothing in their hotel rooms connected them to the crimes.

There were a few international arms dealers that she interacted with at the conference. Sergei Bodrovi, the well-known surface-to-air missile representative. Sergei provided the tools so that others could do the killing. He was the purveyor of death and horror, the man responsible for the killing of entire families, towns, and more. All he cared for were his luxuries. Take away his money or network, and all that was left was a shell of a man who sold his soul to the devil, spending his life drinking champagne and walking on the bones of his victims. He was psychopathic through and through, with the charm to seduce and threaten all at once. She knew when she met him that he was the kind of person that would look into her history; she only hoped her Dream Team created a believable back-story that could handle the scrutiny.

Next was the Lebanese-born Hezbollah operative, Mr. Ali Amin. Unfortunately, his brother had not been at the meeting. She would have enjoyed meeting him. He was the more handsome of the two.

Then there was an international arms trafficker, Ukraine-born Mr. Leonid Minin. Eve believed he had been sent to prison in Italy. He was one with skills that she want- ed to remember. In addition to his skills in arms dealing and forging documents, Minin was also a well-known art thief. His were not the skills you would expect to find all in one person.

All three of the arms dealers were overseas, and Eve did not have the budget nor the time to find out if they were somehow involved.

There were three names she could cross off the list. Joseph Carvallo was an undercover FBI Special Agent that Eve killed to protect her father. He had been at the conference working undercover to seek her out because he knew only through Eve would be able to get to her father. The Tres Piedras village had come together to help John and Eve when Special Agent Carvallo came to town sniffing around. Vic Stallion and Nadia Katz were the other two.

Both Vic and Nadia remained close to Eve, and if either of them had sent the photos...well, she would just give up ever trusting anyone again. Could either of them have done it? Absolutely. Could they have done it and still maintained a closeness with her? Highly unlikely. Eve was not only a trained FBI agent; she had a degree in psychology and had honed her skills at reading people over a lifetime. It would take a master manipulator to pull something like that on Eve.

At IDEC, there was that minor incident in the 3D simulation game when she compromised her cover. Still, Eve wasn't going to go there. If she continued like that, everyone at the conference would be considered a suspect.

Her list of conference-goers was made, and she was just three beers in. Now Eve had to focus on people she knew before the conference. One name came to mind above all others, Aaron Racher. Aaron had been Eve's boyfriend and was an FBI analyst. He was genuinely furious with her when she balked at his almost-marriage proposal, and as an FBI analyst, he had the means to track her. But as FBI, if he found out that she killed people and blew up a building, he would have her indicted. She seriously doubted he would try to blackmail her. Eve didn't really know if she was being blackmailed; she just presumed. The photos were not accompanied by a note or anything disclosing the photographer's motivation.

In college, a few relationships may not have ended as well as they could have. There was Jim, an incredibly nice guy from Clinton, Iowa. He had an extreme phobia of playing music in public, even though he was very talented. Then there was Judy. She was from an ultra-conservative family with a religious ideology that forbade same-sex marriage and preached that all homosexuals were destined for hell. Jim and Judy attached themselves to Eve, dependent on her emotional support, and she had helped both of them overcome their fears. In the end, Eve believed they were better off, but she had left. Was that enough for them to come after her like this?

Dr. Alastair FitzHerbert was the last one to make her list. He had been one of her professors, and when Eve was no longer a student in his class, the two had become friends-with-benefits. Alastair understood Eve. He was like the male version of her. What he offered in his class was everything that made Eve want to study Psychology. Alastair taught his students how to recognize power and control and claim it for themselves. They spent their idle time together playing manipulative games on unsuspecting assholes.

Late one night, they had been particularly successful at humiliating an entitled and belligerent young man causing a ruckus at a bar. When they left, the man followed them in his car, and Alastair drove at high speeds to evade him. He ended up in an accident. Rather than help the guy, they fled. Alastair feared being arrested for drinking and driving, and though Eve was no longer in his class, she was still a student. He had a reputation to uphold. She never saw Alastair after that night and had no idea how to find him. Could he be after her?

She never did find out if the guy following them had lived or died. Maybe he was the one out for revenge? Eve replayed the scene in her head. The car went off the road and flipped as it went down into the ravine. Had they stopped to help, maybe they could have gotten him out of the car. The car caught fire as they drove away.

Eve would like to see Jim and Judy again, but she preferred to keep her distance from Alastair. Eve was not one to get emotionally attached. She just wanted to exert power over people for good, not evil, so she always told herself. However, Eve was very good at seeing into a person and pushing them toward what she believed was best for them. She treated her relationships like the experiments she performed when working on her psychology degree.

Eve reviewed her list and was proud of herself: four years of her life, and she had upset only two people. Not bad. She crossed Alastair off the list.

There was only one person in her life, before college, whom she felt deserved an apology. That would be pudgy Karl. At just twelve years old, Eve wanted to help him overcome his fear of heights. She knew Karl liked her and would do anything for her, so a bargain was made. If he made it to the top of the water tower, she would owe him a kiss. Halfway up the tower, Karl froze. There he was, trembling and crying. Eve judged him as weak and urged him to continue. Karl fell and broke his leg. Eve realized that Karl could have been killed. She also knew that she should have felt something like grief, regret, or sympathy. Instead, all Eve felt was power. Eve knew that with power came great responsibility; she had read all the Spiderman comics when she was young. Karl surely could not have been following her all these years. Eve chuckled.

Her list was complete. Dr. Nicole Mathers would visit Campbell, Elaine, and Rafael from Jamaat al-Fuqura, the Aryan Nation compound, and Payton from the New York Four. FBI Special Agent Eve would visit Jim, Judy, and Aaron. If time permitted, a quick visit to Karl. She was sure apologizing to him, if nothing else, would be beneficial to her, somehow.

Geography and availability would determine the next steps on the path to finding the person behind the photos. Eve had to make sure they could not share the information with anyone else. She went inside, handed her list to her father, and said her good-nights. Three weeks to solve this, what could go wrong?

Chapter Four

ELF Man

Prior to meeting with any of the terrorists from the International Arms conference, Eve had to brush up on her Dr. Nicole Mathers persona. Unfortunately, she hadn't done a good job the first time around: forgetting critical background information and substituting her own. Eve convinced others that she had done this to ingratiate herself with the terrorists, but, in truth, she simply forgot to share the false background her team of FBI experts had created.

The first person on the list was the ELF man

himself, Campbell Greene. He was a member of the Eco terrorist organization, Environmental Liberation Front (ELF). Campbell was also an opinionated, great-earth, vegan hippie. He reminded Eve of a younger version of her father. Both men were very passionate about their beliefs, regardless of the U.S. government's ideological views. In his own words, "There's a line most Americans are not willing to cross. I am."

During their interview, he never admitted to doing anything illegal; however, considering he was on the FBI's list of most wanted, she was confident he was involved in the four-day protesting of the World Trade Organization meetings in Seattle. Thousands had been injured and property damaged. When Campbell spoke of the event, his eyes shone with enthusiasm. Moreover, he spoke with such detail that Eve knew he had participated.

She enjoyed Campbell and looked forward to their conversations and texts. The last time the two had spoken, he announced his new position as a high school science teacher at a very avant-garde school in Portland. So it felt very natural for Eve to give him a call and tell him of a work event taking place at Portland State and invite him to dinner at the *Blossoming Lotus*.

Campbell was one of the people to whom she had revealed her personal childhood during the IDEC interviews and not the Nicole Mathers one explicitly scripted for them. She told him about growing up in the commune and her father being outspoken, anti-government, and wishing for a socialist society. Eve believed her slip up cemented the connection that they had the one that made Campbell invite her to dinner at the end of their interview.

The FBI spent a quarter of a million dollars so Eve could form these relationships. Therefore, when the need arose, she could connect with one of the six hand-selected cells, thanks in part to arms-dealer-turned-informant Vic Stallion. The assortment of terrorists interviewed included both internationally and domestically aligned terrorists. The FBI selected people for her to interview based on their allegiance, ideology, political, and religious goals. Eve was certain that sharing her own personal background had helped with the FBI agenda.

After the interview with Campbell, the two shared a vegan meal, not Eve's first choice in dining options, but she was undercover after all. He made it evident that his interest in her went beyond dinner. She had skillfully evaded his advances, and they went their separate ways at the end of the evening.

Eve noticed that Campbell had evolved over the past three years. He no longer came across as hostile or angry. This reminded Eve of a philosophy that she, or rather Dr. Nicole Mather's FBI team, coined the Born-Again Effect. She was pretty impressed with herself for remembering this.

The Born-Again Effect was a term used to refer to the phenomenon of behavioral changes that manifest when an individual becomes affiliated with a new ideology. This type of change occurs when one is introduced or reintroduced to a religion. Young people leaving home are especially vulnerable. The newfound freedom when a young adult escapes their parents' influence and can explore and choose their own affiliations can be a potent intoxicant. They often initially take their newfound faith or ideology over the top, become extreme in their views, and are less tolerant of people who believe differently.

People under the influence of this phenomenon may limit themselves to being in the company of like-minded individuals or try to recruit or "save" others. Then, after a few years, they taper off, level out, and become less radical. Eve had seen this with people when they quit smoking, drinking, or when they started following a new fad diet. She had not personally witnessed it with religion, but she was undoubtedly aware of born-again Christians and religious extremists.

Before the IDEC conference, the FBI had hired a fashion coach to remake Eve's image. Her coach took her shopping, built her wardrobe, and told her what to wear and when to wear it; basically, a Miss Congeniality makeover. At that time, Eve's personal style could not be considered a style. Her clothes had just one purpose. She dressed to hide in the shadows, to be unknown, unnoticed, and did not deal with all the trappings of feminine fashion. Instead, Eve depended on her playbook assembled by her coach, complete with detailed photos of each ensemble and detailed how-to instructions for putting together a "look," including hairstyle and makeup. Dr. Mathers had it going on.

Eve had worn a simple summer floral print dress with a flared skirt and pockets for her dinner date with Campbell. The pockets really sold it for her. She refused to wear heels, which was fine for this outfit because all she needed was a simple pair of flats. As far as hairstyle, she blew it out straight and used just enough hair product to keep it under control. Eve was comfortable and skipping makeup, a preferred choice of hers. The look had been perfect for an evening with a "greenie" like Campbell.

Eve knew she was fortunate that they allowed her to keep all the clothes from the conference. It was those clothes that she tossed into her suitcase for this trip. She planned to sort them later.

Eve concocted a reason for her to be in Portland that Campbell would believe: she was giving an Introduction to Terrorism presentation at Portland State. She gave herself enough time in advance to explore the university to get a feel of the place. Eve also looked online at the school leadership in case he asked. She was proud of her cleverness. Who needs a team?

Rather than having Campbell choose the restaurant, Eve did a Yelp search and found the Blossoming Lotus. The restaurant had wonderful reviews on their raw and vegan cuisine, so she knew it would satisfy him. Choosing the location herself left Eve in control of the evening, in case he was the one responsible for the photos.

Campbell watched Nicole scan the room before focusing on him. He presumed she wouldn't be prepared for his new look and probably didn't immediately recognize him.

Eve had friend-like feelings for Campbell, so the warm sensations that came over her upon seeing him sitting at the table were surprising. As she approached the table, he stood up, and the change was noticeable. Gone was the T-shirt-wearing extremist she had met at IDEC, and before her was a grown man with purpose.

Campbell had learned that he could compromise, procuring a real job while still caring about things that mattered to him, like the environment and the fight for mother earth. As a high-school teacher, he could enlighten future generations. His professional transition included a short haircut, no piercings, and only a few exposed tattoos.

He not only stood for Eve, but pulled out her chair like a perfect gentleman. Those types troubled her. Never before had Eve met a truly perfect gentleman. Jim, an ex-boyfriend from college, may have been close, and Campbell was no Jim. Someone who appeared this perfect made Eve believe he either had something to hide or was more interested in her than she understood. Eve wasn't sure which one she wanted to be true; having something to hide could be interesting, but she knew if he were enamored with her, he'd be less likely to black-mail her.

A young female server looking as vegan as one can, *you know the look, like she's never eaten meat or anything unhealthy in her life*, zigzagged over in a dress so short that it left nothing to the imagination. Her heels were impractical for someone on their feet all day, but she likely knew what they did for her figure. Eve took solace in the fact that the girl's feet would be aching later and envisioned the bunions she would experience as she aged. Her vegan face was fixed with a peppy false smile. She pulled a pencil from behind her ear, looked directly at Campbell, ignored Eve, and asked about his drink preference. At one point, the overly friendly server's hand rested on his shoulder as she waited for him to respond.

Her overly perky demeanor and obvious flirtation with Campbell caused Eve to daydream about reaching up and choking her dainty little neck. Internally, her mind was wreaking havoc, but Eve maintained a look of calm on the surface. She even donned her own face smile. But, by God, she knew how to fake it; four years in the psychology department had taught her something.

"Eve, they have a specialty drink I think you'll enjoy; do you mind if I order it for both of us?"

She gave Campbell a nod of approval, so he ordered the Goodnight Sweetheart, a drink made with Bourbon, Lime, Ginger Beer, and Bitters. Eve looked down at the menu and noticed the price, only seven dollars for a cocktail. Eve could not remember the last time she had a drink that only cost seven dollars. *Hell, most coffees cost more than seven dollars back home in New York.* Eve would never think of Mobile, Alabama, as home.

Eve inquired about his new job and watched his face light up. He loved teaching the kids and called it a "transforming experience" and said he "learned from them as much as they learned from him." Eve almost felt envious of his role as an educator by the way his eyes sparkled and how animated he became when speaking about his students. She thought maybe someday, when done with this maternity leave, and back in the good graces of her SAC, she should go undercover as a teacher or professor at a University. That would be fun. As long as the students were not entitled little pricks.

When Campbell asked what brought her to Portland, she already had a story in place, but then he asked about her life, and she wasn't prepared for that. Eve stumbled a bit, and she was pretty sure he noticed. Suddenly, she remembered she was supposed to be an academic, a university professor. *Damn, I really suck at this.*

She quickly recovered, took a big drink, coughed, and suggested they order. Eve gave herself time to think up some plausible answers.

Eve scanned the menu. Although she identified as a true-blue meat-eater, she was intrigued by the options listed. Finally, she decided on a cheeseburger, but this wasn't just any old cheeseburger. This was a lentil walnut burger with nut cheese, mixed greens, dried tomatoes, red onion, and avocado. Campbell decided to get a Bibimbap. *I know what you're thinking; what the hell is that?* The dish was full of imposing ingredients like baby bok choy, marinated mushrooms, and ginger-fermented cabbage.

To Eve, it looked to be nothing more than an elaborate coleslaw. As an appetizer, they decided on live nachos. Eve pictured tiny nacho chips with bouncy legs, running around the table, dipping themselves into salsa and guacamole, then jumping into their mouths, satisfying their taste buds with a hint of spiciness. *Viva la' Nacho! Am I the only one who went there?* A smile played at the corners of her mouth. Eve leaned back in her chair and looked at Campbell over the table. She was enjoying herself.

The food was delicious, and the flavors reminded her of the food in Tres Piedras. The two ended up sharing bites of their meals with one another. The lentil walnut burger did not taste one bit like a juicy beef hamburger. Still, Eve found it to be an enjoyable substitute. She expected the meat to be missing from the menu, but she hadn't imagined desserts would be unavailable. There wasn't a single one on the menu. *But, honestly, who eats like this?*

The closest they came to desserts was a variety of smoothies. She truly wanted a warm double chocolate cake with caramel and nuts, with just a hint of vanilla. Still, because there was nothing remotely like that on the menu, she opted for a Hot Date. The Hot Date was made from raw pecans, banana, almond milk, protein powder, dates, cayenne, and cinnamon. Campbell had a Green Dream: spinach, kale, avocado, mango, orange juice, dates, almond butter, and almond milk. The smoothie was no substitute for cake, but like the hamburger, she was experiencing an out-of-the-ordinary alternative. They requested another round of drinks and continued the conversation.

The food offered Eve plenty of time to develop a story to satisfy Campbell's curiosity and reveal if he was involved with the photos.

"Campbell, now that I've had a bit to eat, shall I tell you more about what I'm doing?"

He pushed his plate to the side and leaned in, "I would love to hear what you've been doing, Nicole."

Observing his body language, she stated, "I'm on sabbatical and in the process of writing a fiction book."

He smiled, reached out, and took her hand, "How exciting, tell me more."

Eve glanced down at his hand, now wrapped around hers, and decided to let it remain. "My book is about an FBI agent that goes rogue and blows up a building on Wall Street."

There was no change in his body language: no micro cues or non-verbals gave him away. Instead, Campbell raised his eyebrows just a little and squeezed her hand, "It sounds interesting; I look forward to reading it." He then said, "Do you think an agent would do something like that? I've met a few, and they seem too strait-laced and 'by-the-book' to me."

She responded with a smile and a shrug.

"I'll buy it as soon as it comes out!" He announced.

Eve knew that was going to be a long wait because there was no book, and there would never be a book. She just wanted to watch him, to see if he reacted in a way that exposed any responsibility for the photos. Instead, his reaction was quite the opposite, revealing only his innocence.

Campbell told Eve they should celebrate their good news with a bottle of wine. He gestured to the vegan server, with a smile, to come to the table. She sashayed across the floor, looking, for all intents and purposes, like she was trying to seduce him with her walk. The vegan girl actually frowned when he asked for a bottle of their finest, and Eve had to squelch a laugh. Minutes later, the bottle was thunked unceremoniously onto the table. Campbell had to remind the girl that it needed to be uncorked. She silently worked the corkscrew, filled their glasses, and walked away without a word. Campbell was oblivious to the girl's disappointment. He moved his seat closer to Eve and showed her photos of his students visiting the Sequoia National Park, telling stories about them, and pointing out all the wonders found in the great Northwest.

The moment their hands first touched, photos had started snapping. Someone was watching the couple, and their close contact, laughter, and hand-holding were not making their observer very happy. Moments later, Campbell's Nissan Leaf was hacked. The unknown stalker was able to open the door and retrieve the vehicle identification number.

After their meal, Campbell escorted Eve back to her hotel and was prepared to walk her to her room and stay for a coffee or the night. Either sounded appealing, but unfortunately for him, neither would be happening. Once they reached the hotel, she coincidentally got a call from her father and had to cut the evening short. She gave Campbell a tight hug and a kiss. Not a simple peck, but a full-on-the-lips, lingering-for-just-a-moment-before-backing-away kind of kiss. Eve covered the phone microphone with her hand and whispered, in a seductive yet raspy late-night voice, quiet enough for her father not to hear, "I'll call you tomorrow," and sent him on his way.

Campbell could not believe his bad luck. He had been chasing this woman for three years and really thought tonight would be his night. He was a man in love. Nicole had hair like the wind, wild and free. Eyes like the ocean, deep and mysterious. Eve's energy, full of adventure, with a spirit that could soar. To Campbell, she was the most attractive being in the universe, and she had shot him down. After some reflection about the evening, he clung to her parting words. Eve said she would call him tomorrow, so maybe he'd convince her to stay longer a day or two, or maybe even a week. He picked up his pace and was feeling hopeful and upbeat when he made it back to his car.

The job was easy. All that was necessary was the car's VIN and downloading the *NissanConnect EV* app. All of Campbell's movements could be tracked with this app and the VIN. As long as the driver remained unaware and did not disable their Nissan CarWings account, a person could remotely stop the car, anywhere, anytime.

After what had been witnessed inside the restaurant and the kiss goodnight at Eve's hotel, there was no question of, "If this was going to happen," only "When." Tonight was as good a night as any.

The traffic was pretty crazy, but he expected that on a Friday night in Portland. Campbell made it onto I84 with little problem, but his car started doing strange things when he was near Burnside Bridge on I5. First, the air conditioner went off; within seconds, the music stopped, and then, without warning, he lost control of the steering wheel. The last thing he thought of when plummeting into the Willamette River was that he would not be answering Eve's call tomorrow, or ever again.

Chapter Five

Jim, the Guitar Guy

Eve woke early and had breakfast: bagel, cream cheese, mixed fruit, yogurt, and a pot of coffee. This was her kind of hotel. All she had to do was put the order form on the doorknob the night before, and it would materialize on time. It included a whole pot of her favorite beverage. She took her time eating and in her preparations to see Campbell. Eve was reasonably confident that he was not involved. He was not the kind of guy that would be sending her the photos; he would confront her. She believed he knew nothing of her true identity and knew she would not need to see him again, but she wanted to. It would not be easy to say goodbye; the dad-on-phone trick only works once.

Eve had texted her ELF man and asked if he would like to go for a walk, but he had not yet responded. After breakfast, when she still had no response, Eve picked up her phone and called, something she did only as a last resort. The phone rang straight through to voice mail.

She planned to take the rental car up to Seattle later in the day. The drive was only three hours, but she left earlier than scheduled when ELF man wouldn't pick up. It surprised Eve to find herself feeling melancholy as she was headed North.

Interstate 5 is the main highway on the west coast. It runs parallel to the Pacific Ocean from Mexico to Canada. I-5 goes through California, Oregon, and Washington. Some well-known cities along its path include: San Diego, Los Angeles, Sacramento, Portland, and Seattle. Between Portland and Seattle, the interstate was too far inland to have a view of the ocean. However, the scenery was still rather spectacular, lush forests, Mount Saint Helen's, and the Space Needle. She ended up renting a Hyundai and not a Jeep. Maybe that was why she felt so off. She wasn't a sedan kind of person.

Eve was on her way to see Jim, Iowa Jim, guitar Jim, all the above. He was, bar none, the nicest, most fantastic guy she had ever known. Eve remembered the day she broke his heart, almost as if it were yesterday. She had been working at a college bar during her junior year, and there he was, ordering an Old Fashioned.

Unbeknownst to her at the time, Jim was in one of her classes at Columbia and had tracked her down, hoping to get a chance to meet her. Jim had striking blue eyes, a mop of messy hair, and a smile so contagious you could not help but smile back.

Jim was a wizard with the guitar. He could make it do things that most could only dream about doing. Eve grew up surrounded by music and knew quality and talent when she heard it. So she was surprised to hear that Jim was so deathly afraid of playing in front of people that he would become physically ill. Eve had been under the impression that people outside her desert commune were socially adapted, with few insecurities, and could function comfortably around strangers. Apparently, this was not the case for everyone, and certainly not for Jim.

Eve and Jim became lovers, and she made him her project. She worked with him and encouraged him with every manipulative tool in her toolbox to get him comfortable playing for an audience. The first step was to encourage him to play guitar only for her. The two of them alone at her place, followed by sex, laughter, and drinks, not necessarily in that order. This was a reward system she designed.

When this became the norm for him, Eve packed a lunch, and they, with his guitar, went to an isolated location within Central Park. The trip to the park was repeated, but the areas in the park were in more populated places. Jim's music began to attract attention, and each time the crowd size increased. The last hurdle was for him to perform at the Columbia students' cool hang out, *Bar 1020*. As a bartender there, she had an 'in' with the owners and could get the space for him to play.

After a round of nausea, and a firm refusal to look at the audience, Jim began to play. He played as if there were no one else in the room, and they loved him. One audience member was particularly enthralled by Jim, that was Wendy, with the green dress.

When Jim's anxiety about playing for an audience was conquered, Eve's interest in him waned. She knew ending it unexpectedly, when for all intents and purposed they looked like a couple in love, was wrong; it hurt him, but she did it anyway. Her sanity and personal space were more important. Some people, okay, most people, would not understand that she did all of this to help him, not to use or play with him. She knew early on that she lacked some of the emotions others experienced.

Eve considered herself a moral person, but that didn't stop her from feeling proud of her skills at manipulation and her ability to use them to control others. She had spent her whole life perfecting those skills, first when trying to fit in around outsiders back home in New Mexico. Then, when adapting to the social structure, she encountered by observing her classmates at Columbia.

It became far more than a hobby. Her Bachelor of Science in psychology increased her knowledge of human behavior and enhanced her skills, as did her training with the FBI. Years before, when poor chunky Karl was injured due to her manipulations, younger Eve had promised herself that her talents would only be used for good, never evil. It had become her personal mantra.

It took little effort to find Jim. His mother used to call so often that Eve knew her number by heart, and true to form, his mom still had it, even after all this time.

Jim's mom was quick to brag about her boy playing in a band in Seattle. He even had his own album. After jotting down the band's name, *Central Park*, Eve said goodbye and hung up the phone, reminding herself once again how much she hated talking on the phone. A good phone would let you do anything, but call others. To reward herself for making a phone call, she picked up a fresh coffee and a Honey Cruller donut at *Tim Hortons*.

A quick Google search provided Eve with everything she needed to know about Central Park and its tour dates. This evening they were playing at *Neumos*. With a seating capacity of 650, Eve was convinced that Jim's fear of playing for an audience was well behind him. Eve checked into the *Silver Cloud Hotel* and took a nap. She was starting to worry. Eve had still not heard from Campbell. He must be really upset with me.

When she was sufficiently awake, she got dressed for the club, downed a cup of coffee, and walked the short walk to the venue, taking Madison to 10th street. The five-minute walk felt refreshing. Eve noted only one coffee shop on the way, but at least five places to eat, including *Monster Dogs*, in case she was hungry on her way back. She knew she would rather have put on an oversized tee and stayed in, but duty called.

When Eve walked into *Neumos*, she was surprised at the size. It had three bars, a mezzanine level, and an exclusive balcony that overlooked the showroom. There was mostly standing room only, but she spotted a couple of dozen seats were hidden away in the mezzanine. For her, the best part of the club was the *Pike Street Fish Fry*, an attached restaurant and part of the Pike Street Fish Market.

Eve ordered a beer and waited until the band was onstage before she maneuvered a spot in the front. She recognized Jim right away and knew when he recognized her because he missed a beat. Their eyes locked, and Eve's breath caught in her throat. She could not take her eyes off him and his smile. Eve just stood there, grinning back, just like the mesmerized fans all around .

At the band's first break Jim found Eve sitting at a table, alone and looking as beautiful as ever. He was overjoyed at seeing her so far from home and gave her a big smile. She motioned to the chair next to her. He sat down, and when the server stopped by, he ordered an Old Fashioned in memory of their first encounter.

"How did you find me?" He inquired.

"I called your mom. She was quite helpful, told me the name of your band. By the way, do you know how proud she is of you?"

"Yeah, she also knows it's all because of you. You're the reason I'm here today; did she tell you that?"

"No," Eve laughed, "But she did say she wanted to cook for me. I think that's mom code for she likes me." She paused for a minute, then said, "Thank you for telling me that my influence on you was positive. To be honest, Jim, I thought you hated me, and I was nervous about showing up."

"Are you kidding? Why do you think the band is called *Central Park*? That's an homage to you," he lifted his drink up to toast her. "I even wrote an album with songs all about our time together. Two of the songs, Apartment on the *Upper West Side* and *Raspberry Filling*, both done very well. You were my muse, Eve, I owe you everything."

Eve could not believe what she was hearing. All these years, she thought he didn't understand her, when he did. Her eyes started to water, and she had to look away, and make an excuse. "Damn, it's scorching in here, I need to get some air." She stood up. "I'll be back soon, Jim. Then we can talk some more."

"I'll have to go back on stage in a few minutes. How about I bring you breakfast in the morning, and we go for a walk?"

"That would be fantastic," Eve grabbed his hand, and a pen from a table's check presenter folio, and wrote her hotel and room number on his arm. She then tossed the pen back onto the table, ignoring the looks the couple sitting there gave her, and worked her way through the crowd to the entrance. Eve was in too good of a mood to notice the people, not even when one nearly toppled her in a hurry to secure a spot near the stage.

She walked back to the hotel and stopped in the lobby for a bag of jellybeans and another of sour worms, then headed up to her room to take a bath and watch some *Netflix*. Eve slept well that night, and the smile never left her face.

She was still in bed when there was a knock on the door. Jim had arrived with coffee and, she couldn't believe it, two big rolls stuffed with eggs, sausage, and cheese. He even remembered the packets of hot sauce. It had been forever since she tasted his mom's recipe: meat, egg, and cheese rolls. He climbed onto the bed with her, and they shared breakfast while talking about their lives.

He was not surprised to find out she had joined the FBI, but married and two kids was too much to wrap his mind around. He was married, too, with a few kids, all of them back in Iowa, with his mom. Unfortunately, Eve wasn't listening closely enough to get all the facts, just the Cliff Notes version.

When breakfast was over, Eve dressed, and they walked around Pike's Market. The hustle and bustle reminded Eve of New York, but the smell was definitely not New York. After the walk, they said their goodbyes and Eve went up to her room to pack and return to her family. Jim and the band stayed at the *Kimpton Alexis Hotel*, a twenty-five-minute walk down Madison. He had to go prepare for another show that night.

If one is interested in electrocuting a musician, by far the easiest way to do this would be to plug the guitar amplifier into an electrical outlet on the stage. The main sound console, to which the microphone is grounded, would be plugged into a different outlet elsewhere. When these two power points are at different ground voltages, a current can flow between the grounded mic's housing and the grounded guitar strings. If the guitar amp and console are on different phases of alternating current mains, things can get dangerous. Arranging such another accident and not being spotted, can be simple. One only need dress up as road crew and act as if they belong.

Jim did not expect a thing when, at the start of the second set, he grabbed the mic in front of him and was electrocuted. He would later learn that the electricity entered the right side of his body and came out of his right foot. If it had gone through the left side, it would have struck his heart and stopped it from beating. Instead, the exit wound left a visible circle on the sole of his foot the size of a quarter.

His jeans had burned to his legs, and his leather jacket disintegrated. Jim's t-shirt was full of burn holes. The shoes he was wearing helped save his life because they had thick rubber soles, but that was all that was left of them, the rest had been burned away. Jim's smile was gone. He was burnt from head to toe, and the doctors said there was only a 25% chance he would make it through the night.

Jim would never be the same. There was no skin on his face. He resembled a cadaver with red raw exposed muscles and veins popping out. The doctor said he would need several skin grafts, up to twenty, all down the right side of his body. If and when Jim was ready to leave the hospital, he would still have to return every day for months to have the bandages changed.

Earlier that morning, Eve drove to *SeaTac* airport,

and dropped off her rental car. She waited for her flight back to Taos inside the airport's marketplace. The space was expansive, with floor-to-ceiling views, along with live trees, giving the illusion that you are outside, but safe from inclement weather. Her flight home was with *American*; 5:50 PM–11:59 PM.

She had time for sushi at the *Koi Shi Sushi Bento* food station within the marketplace and a *Starbucks* coffee chaser. Both would tide her over. It would be late when she got back to Tres Piedras, but she knew food and her family would be waiting for her. She missed Harper chatting her ear off and holding baby Franklin. This was the longest she had been apart from them both, and the longing she felt to be back with her children made her feel almost human.

She needed to go back to her dad's and prepare for her trip to Charlotte County, Virginia, and the Jamaat al-Fuqura. Eve was very aware that going to the al-Fuqura compound would be dangerous, she would have to keep on her toes.

It surprised Eve to see Nadia waiting for her at the airport. Eve had traveled light when she went north, leaving the bulk of her luggage and her children at her father's. So with just her carry-on, Eve was able to bypass the baggage claim and head straight out.

When Nadia saw Eve walking past the security, she noticed a glow about her, a look of contentment. Maybe she was wrong about Eve and married life, maybe being married to Franklin was good for Eve. Then again, her look could mean something entirely different, Nadia mused, it had to be sex, she knew intuitively, Eve had sex with one of the guys she just visited, hopefully, Jim, oh please, please be Jim. Nadia took a deep breath. The news she was about to tell Eve would be heart-breaking.

Nadia gave Eve a hug, "It's wonderful to see you, and you look amazing." She grabbed Eve's carry-on and put it over her shoulder. Eve lifted an eyebrow and gave her a smirk. She could carry her own damn bag, but not having it on her shoulder was a nice break, so she let it go. They made their way through the terminal and headed to the short-term parking.

Nadia did not miss the eyebrow or the smirk, "What? It's late; you've been on a plane all day."

Eve ignored the comment, and gave her a once over look, "Hey, Nadia, it's good to see you, life in the desert seems to be working for you."

"It does have its benefits." She nudged Eve's shoulder with her own. "Not least of all, your father."

Eve rolled her eyes and changed the subject. "So, everyone good? I know; I've only been gone three days."

They reached Nadia's car, one Eve had not seen before. "A new car. I guess you had to get rid of the other one?"

When FBI Special Agent Carvallo used Eve to find her father, his desire to get his man at any cost led him to John's door. His insistence on getting into their home, using his badge and weapon, meant he was not long for this world. Nadia had knocked him out, and with the help of a physician in the village, his death was ruled an accident. However, Eve knew that Nadia's car could have implicated her. There was a chance that someone saw the vehicle at the site where the agent's car took a tumble into a ravine, so she sold it. Eve replaced that beautiful car with an old 2001 white with black interior (in a desert?) Discovery Land Rover. What was she thinking? That must be expensive as hell to repair.

Once they got on the road, Nadia told Eve the bad news. "Eve, your dad told me about your 'mission,' and he also shared with me that he put alerts on his computer so that the people on your list show up anywhere on the Internet, he gets a notice."

"That was a great idea, but why do you sound upset? Did he find something?"

"Yes. Campbell Greene, the teacher you met within Oregon two days ago, was in a car accident and died; I'm really sorry."

"That explains why he never returned my texts or emails. When did it happen? Was it alcohol-related?" He did have a lot to drink that night. She was sure he was clear-headed when he left her. Besides, the walk back to the car should have sobered him up.

"It happened the night you two met. Your dad will retrieve any autopsy reports if they do one. He's been monitoring the incident for the last day or so."

"Well, I had already crossed him off the suspect list, which is too bad. Had he been the one that sent the photos, this would all be over." Eve sounded for all the world as if she would like it to be over and that her life could return to normal. Yet, she was secretly relieved that Campbell was not responsible for the photos, her skills at reading people were still strong. The mystery continues, and she has more adventures ahead of her.

"How are the kids? Have Mari's girls, I forgot their names, have they helped Mari with Harper and Franklin?

"The girls, Jada and Rose, are helping their mom. But, really, Eve, you need to keep up; they are practically family, you know your terrorists better than you do the good people in your life."

Once again, Eve did not like where the conversation was heading. She turned on the Rover's CD player and looked out the window. Nadia knew they were done talking.

Shortly after midnight, the two pulled into the drive.

Eve's dad was standing at the door, with it propped open. "Hi Dad, anything new?" She asked him while she kissed his cheek.

"Nope, come inside. Do you want coffee or to just go to bed?" He asked them both.

Neither wanted coffee, and Eve made her way back to the bedroom. The girls doubled up, so Eve and Harper shared a room and a bed. Mari had Franklin in with her. After a quick shower and brushing her teeth, extra-long on the tooth brushing, Eve always felt extraordinary unclean after traveling. Finally, she got into bed, pulled her daughter close, and fell asleep.

Eve woke feeling like she had been in a war, then

she remembered her daughter had slept with her, and the battle wounds she was feeling were due to Harper's habit of kicking and moving around all night. She believed Harper elbowed her in the face at one point, but it could have been a dream.

She could have sworn Camilla was still with them when she walked into the kitchen. The smell of breakfast surrounded her: chorizo sizzling in the pan, baked eggs, fresh-squeezed orange juice, and coffee. She was surprised to see everyone was already awake.

A table with enough chairs to feed a tribe, that was what Camilla insisted on when she moved in. Eve sat down and ran her hand across the smooth tabletop. She had such fond memories of this table, great food, her father present, sober, and happy neighbors stopping by.

She remembered the time when she was eleven or twelve, and Camilla caught her carving her initials into the side. Her fingers found the deep scratches. Eve told Camilla she wanted to be remembered forever. She didn't get into trouble for it. Camilla had just patted her on the shoulder and said, 'Next time, find a tree outside.'"

After breakfast, Eve took her freshly-topped-off cup of coffee, laptop, and cell phone outside. After glancing at her watch, she knew it was time to check in with Franklin and the office. She fully expected her husband to be upset, having not spoken to him since they started their trip. But, instead, when his voice-mail picked up, the relief felt was palpable. Eve didn't want to lie to him, but she wasn't about to share what she had really been up to.

"Hi Franklin, sorry I didn't call earlier, we've been swamped, and I'm just now getting a chance to relax. Mari and Nadia made a fantastic breakfast, and I am about to take the kids to town. The neighbors couldn't get enough of them on our first night here. Chat soon, bye." Eve realized she hadn't said she loved him when she ended the call. Dammit.

Eve had not given any thought to Campbell being dead, it seemed a little too surreal, and she did not have the time to concern herself with something that couldn't be changed. However, she did recall the beverage she had at the *Blossoming Lotus* and wondered if her dad had the ingredients to make one here. If not, they could always pick some things up when she went into town.

The process of logging into her work laptop through a PVN was tedious. If they made it more accessible, she would probably check it more often. Her email address was easy to remember, emblack@fbi.gov; however, her password was not. Eighteen letters, numbers, symbols, some upper case, some lowercase, she knew the importance of everything being secure, but what a pain. Eve never used her email for anything not directly related to work. The security filters were cumbersome. Only select email addresses could send to you, and the attachments had to go through some approval process. Her father could explain it, if she were really interested. She found it much easier to use her personal email.

Thirty-three new messages on the FBI mail server. It

may sound like a small number after such an absence, but considering the restrictions, she knew there would likely not be any junk email in the bunch. She did a quick glance down the list; one stood out. The subject was ELF. Eve opened it. Bloody hell.

No words, just photo attachments. Photos of Campbell and Eve at the restaurant laughing, one with him holding her hand, and one of the two of them walking to her hotel late at night. She did not find those photos particularly shocking. However, the next photo caused Eve to convulse. It was an image of Campbell's car, with his broken and bloody body still inside, sinking into the river well before the ambulance or police arrived. Not only did Eve feel sick, but it also left her dumbfounded, asking herself how, and more importantly, who?

All the blood drained from her face. Eve felt light-headed, and her pulse sped up. She looked around at the drive, the water tower across the street, and the neighbors. They could be out there right now. Her weapon was inside, and so were her children. She had to protect them above all else.

Eve walked inside and immediately called a family meeting. Mari asked the teens to take her children to their rooms, so the grownups could talk. They did so without question, but the pout on their faces let everyone know they felt they should be allowed to stay. Eve thought to herself that she really should remember the girls' names. Eve knew one was Rose, but which one, she had no idea.

Eve was comfortable talking business in front of

Mari. She had, after all, been there when Mari killed her two brothers-in-law, two verbally and sexually abusive men that had twisted plans for her daughters. She opened her email and showed them all the photos.

"Forward this to my Proton email account," John said firmly, "There's a chance I can check the IP and inspect the photos to see if they came from the same camera as the photos sent to you in the mail. Don't concern yourself too much Evie. We'll figure this out, I promise you." John was becoming terribly concerned, but he was not going to tell his daughter this.

Eve found it endearing that he reverted to her childhood nickname when her dad felt emotional toward her. She forwarded the email and then announced, "There's no way I can go to the al-Fuqura compound now. I can't just leave my children here, leave all of you here; not when someone is playing games like this."

Nadia looked directly at Eve and said, "Seriously, Eve, do you think we can't handle ourselves or that I can't protect them? You've seen me fight, right?" Without giving Eve a chance to interject, she continued, "This may be the safest place on earth for them to be. We have the town watchdogs, a stash of weapons, and experience. If something goes down, we'll send the kids to the bunker and kick some ass."

Mari nodded in agreement, "Eve, I wouldn't want my girls anywhere else. This is the safest place I know. We'll take care of your babies; you need to find out who's doing this."

"We will just make a plan," Nadia then left the

room. No one said a word, they just looked around, and finally, John started humming the theme song to Jeopardy. Nadia was back in no time and handed Eve a new phone. "It's new, it's encrypted, and I can find the owner of this phone through GPS, no matter where they are in the world."

This was not the time to ask Nadia where she got the phone or why she had it, so she nodded and said, "Thanks."

"Every six hours, you will click on this icon."

Eve was happy to see an easily identifiable, a six-pointed star replacing the hands of a clock.

"If you go more than six hours between clicking on the icon, I will receive an alert and your last known coordinates. If you get in trouble, and you have the ability, you need to click on this nearly identical icon," She pointed to a six-pointed star embedded in a compass, "It will send an alert to my phone, telling me that you're in trouble and again, show your GPS coordinates. Can you keep that straight?"

She glanced over at Eve, hoping for a response, a glimmer of understanding. Instead, what she got from Eve was a loud sigh, a narrowing of her eyes, and a crossing of her arms. Yep, she understood.

"If you cannot click on it, and more than six hours pass, know that I will be on my way. I'll come to get you, and Eve, this is what I'm trained to do. I know you are FBI, but that's law enforcement, not search and rescue. I'll find you and bring you home. I give you both my word."

At that time, Harper bounced into the room and said, "Me too, me too, mommy," without knowing what was going on. The timing was perfect and just what was needed to lighten the mood. They all laughed, and the tension was lifted.

Nadia leaned over and whispered to Eve, "I need you to call Vic and tell him to stash some weapons near the AF compound that I can retrieve if I need to."

Then, looking in John's direction, "John, make sure we have an up-to-date list of flights if we have to move fast."

"Yes, ma'am!" He quipped.

She gave him a smile and then addressed Mari. Mari leaned forward, ready to do her part.

"You need to guarantee that Eve is well fed and has plenty of coffee; you know how she gets!"

Mari nodded. "And I need both you and John to ensure that her children are taken care of while she's gone. They should be the last thing she has to worry about."

This time Nadia's direction was focused on Eve, "This is likely to be the most dangerous mission you've experienced. You'll have to keep your focus, not drop cover. We know how you can get, and frankly, I'm really concerned about you. You can not mess this up."

Eve just nodded her head. She knew Nadia was right. The priority was finding out who was behind the photos. She texted Rafael to confirm her arrival and went back to the room to prepare. Her bag was light.

The mission would be quick, the go-in, interview, and get-out kind. What she did need was some alone time to process. John headed to the bunker to see what he could find out. Nadia decided to do a perimeter walk, and Mari invited the kids to help her make cookies.

That evening, Eve went outside so she wouldn't have the others listening and made a phone call to Vic.

"Hey, doll face, what's up?" Vic said, sounding very Jersey, an accent that had become something of an inside joke between the two.

"Vic, I need your help again."

His voice instantly took on a more serious tone, "What's going on, Eve?"

"I'm being blackmailed, and I haven't been able to figure out who's doing it. They have photos." She paused, but for just a second, "A few days ago, one of the terrorists from the conference, you know which one," best not to assume the phone was secure, she reminded herself, a bit too late, "I went to see him two days ago, and shortly after I left him, he was killed, and by the person that sent me the photos. So I can't go into too much detail. My dad and Nadia are helping, but we need weapons stashed outside the AF compound, just in case it's them."

"Eve, honey, slow down, I'm not following you."

She calmed herself and started over. "Last week photos showed up at my house, in an envelope, photos of me in a very compromised fashion."

"Compromised?"

Fine, screw the phone line. "I killed a couple people, planted a bomb, and framed Jackson and his friends, and someone took photos."

"I knew you were up to something, but I had no idea what." Then, after a short pause, he added, "What can I do?"

She knew she could count on Vic; that's why she called him. Eve told him their Plan B, and Nadia's role as a backup. She explained that Nadia would be unable to bring her own weapons because she would need to fly on a commercial airlines.

"Not a problem, Eve; I'll have the weapons ready and will text you the location. You need anything else from me?"

"No, I think that's it."

"I'm hanging up now and will work out some details. I'll text you before you get on the plane tomorrow; how's that?"

"That's great. I really appreciate it."

"Not a problem, not a problem at all. You know I've got your back."

Chapter Six

Oh Fuqura

Eve showed up at the compound wearing dark blue jeans, a faded gray cotton tee, a midnight gray Eddie Bauer travel blazer, and her Franco Sarto Loafers leftover from the FBI makeover. When she made it to the gate guard's post, Eve gave them her name, Dr. Nicole Mathers, and followed their directions to a park. She left her bag in the rental car and walked up to the Elder's house, a blue, one-story, double-wide trailer with a wooden make-shift porch that threatened to fall apart with each step. Eve knocked and was happy to see Elaine answer the door. Elaine had not changed in the three years, she still looked ageless and elegant. Her statuesque form and posture would lead you to believe she was a supermodel or a person of wealth and class, not someone living in a derelict compound in the middle of nowhere. While her attire included a traditional African print dress, she also wore a tightly fitted head wrap in the Muslim style. She smiled at Eve and said, "Hello, Dr. Mathers, it's so good to see you again. My husband, Rafael, is on his way. May I offer you some tea or coffee?" She gestured Eve inside.

The trailer had aged wood paneling on the walls, an Amish table surrounded by several sturdy wooden chairs, and more chairs throughout the room against the walls. The kitchen area was small but clean, and the smell of coffee made the space tolerable. An orange sofa with green velvet pillows was on one side of the trailer, reminding Eve of the seventies. She expected that they would sit there and was unpleasantly surprised when Elaine guided her not to the sofa but to the chairs closest to the kitchen, requiring Eve to have her back to both the entry door and the hallway leading back to what she could only assume were the bedrooms and bath.

She was grateful that Elaine reminded her to use her pseudonym. Eve likely would not have remembered to do so. "Coffee would be lovely, Elaine, and please, call me Nicole."

Eve heard a male voice behind her, "Why would we call you Nicole when your name is Evelyn? Evelyn Black, or should I say, FBI Special Agent Evelyn Black?"

"Bloody Hell," Eve said to herself in a voice barely audible, she quickly stood and turned around to face

Rafael and a few other AF men. Eve thought Rafael was a big man, but he was pretty average compared to his two buddies. Muslim and African-American, all three were dressed in traditional Muslim attire, ankle-length garments with long sleeves, similar to a tunic. On their heads were taqiyahs, short, rounded skullcaps. They looked imposing, not gentle or peaceful like most men did when dressed in this fashion. Eve started to speak, and Rafael quickly shut her up by slapping her across the face so hard she fell backward over her chair, falling to the floor.

"Oh, my husband," Elaine said to Rafael, "I wanted to offer her some coffee and give her a personal tour of the compound before you started with the torture."

She gave an exaggerated sigh and shook her head as if it were merely a slight inconvenience that her plans were changed. Elaine looked down at Eve as she was attempting to stand. "Agent Black, I would advise you to stay down."

Eve ignored her warning and attempted to get back up. That was when Rafael kicked her in the stomach, and Eve fell back to the ground. She couldn't breathe and hunched over, warding off another kick to the gut. Feeling exposed and vulnerable, Eve was glad she had not eaten anything since early that morning, or she would have lost it.

Eve tried to crawl away but was surrounded by six men at once, and they looked quite intimidating. She curled up into a ball and closed her eyes. Eve would have to wait this one out; either they would kill her, or Nadia would rescue her. There were no other options. She had just checked in before arriving, so Eve knew she had to survive six hours, plus a plane ride and a driving time to get here. Twelve hours at the most. She could do it.

The blows kept coming, and the pain compounded as her body's bruised and broken areas were intentionally kicked or hit repeatedly. She was sure her ribs were cracked, if not broken. Eve felt a popping sensation in her knee, and there was an unbearable throbbing, especially when she tried to move her leg. The blows left her feeling lightheaded. There were black spots and white flashes in her vision. A kick to the head caused a ringing in her ears, and then she passed out.

When she came to, the air was thick with the scent of fresh-brewed coffee. Eve was strapped to a chair with duct tape, and there was a mug of hot coffee in front of her. Unable to reach out and pick up the mug, she thought to herself, that's the real torture. Fuck them. Eve tried to lean forward to reach it with her tongue, just a small taste..., impossible.

She was having trouble seeing. Both eyes were swelled almost shut. Blood had pooled in her mouth and leaked out between her teeth. Her mouth was too dry to allow her saliva to dissolve the metallic crud. A wound on her head was still bleeding. She could feel the blood running down her face. Eve wished it would stop, that they would stop. She just needed a minute to think, to plan an escape. Her ears were ringing, and the voices coming at her sounded like they were in a tunnel.

Rafael's facial expression was one of absolute disdain. He despised her. She meant nothing to him. "Tell us why you're here. What's the mission, Agent

Black?" Rafael inquired.

She would not provoke him with phrases like "Go to hell" or "Go fuck yourself." Agents did this all the time and the only thing it got them was more pain. Or at least that's how it happened on TV. Although, come to think of it, she didn't know any agents personally that had ever been tortured, hmmm... a first, go her! And she smiled a big bloody grin.

The next blow to her face was hard, and this time he used a closed fist. She felt her nose crack, and blood spurted onto her white tee. Damn, she loved that tee. It would likely never come clean again. She thought about the man on the plane and how she tripped him, God, she could use a Bloody Mary, hah, a bloody Bloody Mary.

"Agent Black, I really don't want to kill you," Rafael growled. He attacked with a big right overhand punch.

Eve tried to dodge, but taped to the chair, she succeeded only in offering her chin to the blow, causing the chair and Eve to fall backward and onto the floor with a thump. She was helped up by two unseen thugs, only to take another fist to the face.

She told herself to keep calm and keep the inner dialog going. Bloody, my favorite phrase is Bloody Hell, why? Oh, from that TV show when I was younger. I decided to make it my catchphrase. Franklin never... another blow to the face, the ringing in her ears changed to a different pitch. Franklin was raised in England and never said Bloody Hell. What was wrong with him? That's when the next fist got her. Eve tried to get up but realized she was still stuck to the chair. How could she forget? Eve bit her lip to keep from crying out. She laid her head back down. Every movement that passed caused some muscle or bone to ache, and her awareness ebbed. Black fog swirled at the edges of her consciousness, drawing her in, and she lost the fight.

When she woke, it was pitch black. It took her some time to remember where she was, somewhere on the al-Fuqura compound. As her eyes grew accustomed to the dark, she could tell she was in a cell with dirt walls, obviously underground. She started to lose her nerve. At least five or six hours had to have passed. Would Nadia find her here? Did they plan to leave her down here? God, she hurt. With her tongue, she felt around her mouth. A few teeth were loose, and one or two were missing. As her eyes adjusted to the dark, she realized the cell was one of many, and she found this oddly reassuring.

Eve knew she had to keep her wits about her if she would get out of this predicament. She closed her eyes and forced herself to open her other senses to describe her current environment. Mold, moisture, and dirt. The smell of the earth was different from the desert sand. That smell is metallic. This is more like potting soil with a sweet smell. There was a bucket in the corner with a few inches of smelly stale water. Its purpose is not for drinking but for bodily functions as a portable toilet. Her captors must not like to clean up human excrement, but she noted they had not provided toilet paper.

Apparently, she had also wet herself. Well, good, being unclean would keep the Muslim men away. Eve was having difficulty focusing. She was hungry, thirsty, and frightened.

86

With nothing to do to occupy her mind, she could only focus on her pain and imminent rescue. She attempted to move when she thought it possible, then realized it made things worse. Eve gritted her teeth and dragged herself closer to the corner, in the back, and knelt, leaning a shoulder against the wall. She knew she would give in. Everyone could be broken, and Eve was no exception. They will do what it would take to break her and before long, she would have to give in, either due to pain or exhaustion. Her thoughts went foggy. She lost consciousness once again and hit the cold dirt floor, her arm breaking the fall.

She woke again to find Rafael sitting on a wooden stool outside the cell, staring at her. In his hand was a glass of crystal-clear water. The glass was a beautiful sight and the water even more so. The dim light was reflected in the condensation and in the droplets that fell to the ground. Drip. Drip. Drip. Eve's mouth was dry, and her lips cracked from lack of liquids. She ran her tongue over her gums, seeking moisture of any kind, trying to dissolve the thick crusty blood, still there from the earlier beating. The was never a time when she wanted water more than she did at that moment, and this was almost comical, considering she was raised in a desert.

She sniffed the air. He smelled of shampoo, soap, and cologne. It must be a new day. He also smelled of tobacco, something forbidden to Muslims, so he was clearly not opposed to breaking some rules. There was another smell she knew very well, gunpowder. The stench wasn't coming from him. She wondered if there was a firing range nearby. "Agent Black, why are you here?"

Again, she kept quiet. Rafael looked to his right and gave someone a nod, one of the men from earlier, or at least she assumed she had seen him then. The men all had beards, long robes, and psychotic looks in their eyes, so she could not be sure. He unlocked the cell, and the two grabbed her arms and dragged her down a path past the other cells. She could not prevent a gasp and moan from escaping her lips. Eve noticed the other cells were empty. Then the pain in her knee made her pass out again. This time she felt it coming and welcomed it.

When Eve awoke, she found herself naked, exposed, and lying on a board. Her body was on an incline, with her feet above her head and a damp cloth on her face, covering her nose and mouth. Eve knew what was coming. She had no experience but had read enough to know she was about to be water-boarded.

That's when the panic began. She struggled and tried to break free of the restraints, thus increasing her pain. Her eyes opened wide with dilated pupils. They darted back and forth, looking for a means to escape. Tears ran down her face, exposing a clean path of skin among the dirt and blood. Her dirty tears pooled in the folds of her ear. Once it started, there was no holding back. Her body convulsed, and the dam was open. "No, this can't be happening. Eve wanted her dad. She tried to call out to him, to scream at the top of her lungs, "Daddy!" But her voice was muffled due to the wet cloth clinging to her mouth. She heard the water before it poured into her upturned mouth and nose. Eve knew she wasn't drowning, but she couldn't distinguish real from unreal.

She tried to breathe in and out, but no air entered her lungs. Starved for oxygen, Eve's heart raced at tremendous speeds. Safety and security were nothing but a distant memory. She closed her mouth and turned her head from side to side, trying to block the stream, but she felt a finger forcing her mouth open, so water flowed freely inside. She swallowed, choked, and coughed spastically. What felt like an eternity was actually only a few seconds. But, on the good side, she was no longer thirsty.

The flow of water stopped, the plank was raised, and she heard a whisper in her ear, "Agent Black, why are you here?"

She didn't respond right away, but when the plank started to lower, she said, in a voice barely audible, "I'm being blackmailed!"

The movement stopped, and the plank began to rise. Eve almost wept with joy, but she knew it could start again at any moment.

"Well, now, that's intriguing." Rafael said, "Tell me more."

"I blew up an insurance company and killed two men." She wanted to say more, but she couldn't. Just the one line took all her energy.

"Keep talking, Agent Black."

She tried again. Eve knew the stakes, "Someone took pictures, I'm trying to find out who."

"It has nothing to do with our weapons stash or plans to blow up Congress?" He asked her in a matter-of-fact way.

She now knew he had no plans to release her. He had just shared their terrorism plot, and telling him she 'promised not to tell' would fall on deaf ears.

The fear she was experiencing made the fogginess dissolve. She had to try to make friends, "No. I don't know what you're talking about. I'm just trying to figure out who was blackmailing me."

"What about the FBI? Do they know you are here?"

She had to think her answer through. If she said yes, would they kill her sooner or later? God, she wished she had some coffee. "No."

"Good answer, Evelyn."

She was shocked to hear Elaine speak, "Raf, put her back in the cell, let her have some sleep. I am sure she will explain it all tomorrow, after a nice breakfast, right, Agent Black?"

At that moment, she wanted to hug Elaine, but instead, she just nodded her head and whispered a "Yes."

When Eve did not check-in, her friends and family knew something was wrong. With Plan B now in place, they entered rescue mode. By the time Nadia got to the airport, John had her ticket waiting, and in just under an hour, she was on the plane. She landed in Virginia seven hours later.

Nadia pushed everyone out of her way as she made it through the terminal and out toward baggage claim. This was going to be a one-woman show, and she was going in blind. She had to waste time getting a car, retrieving the weapons, and then driving to a compound, where she would have to deal with an unknown number of armed men and women.

She knew she could do this. This is what she had spent the last decade training for, but the stakes had never been this high, nor had she ever been back up.

When she passed security, she saw a man, looking less like a driver and more like a military soldier, holding up a sign with her name. Underneath her name, the sign read Courtesy of Vic Stallion. She smiled and quickly walked over to him.

He told Nadia that Vic had sent him in to fetch her. She nodded her understanding. He turned and walked toward the exit. Right outside the airport's exit was a black SUV. She knew that since 9/11, parking that close to the terminals was strictly forbidden. She had no idea how he managed it, but at the moment, she didn't care. She got inside the vehicle, handed the man the GPS coordinates, and he, in turn, handed her an earpiece. She took it, and as soon as she inserted it into her ear, she heard an unfamiliar male voice discussing the plans.

"All, fifty-minute ETA. Time check, 0448. We're taking Thomas Jefferson Highway to Rolling Hill road. We think the compound is spread out over several farms. Team one, you turn right on Gilani Lane and secure that home. Team two, second road on the left past Gilani Lane, secure that space, two buildings there. Teams three, four, and five, take the next right, you will see one building, secure that building, that's home base. Mission parameters, it's kill first, question later. When pre-mission is complete, teams one and two join us at the home base. If we can't bring Starbucks out alive, the mission is a red wash. Team one and two, verify membership before killing. Everyone got this? The team leaders all responded sequentially with a "roger."

Nadia's driver took her directly to the home base. He must have slowed down, or one of the other teams sped up because the home base was already secure when they got there. Nadia got out of the SUV and saw Vic with at least ten other men dressed for war.

"Okay, team, everyone over here," came a voice Nadia knew to be Vic over the earpiece.

"We did a recon of the place," he pulled out a map, "Based on the GPS cords and Intel, we believe she's..." he pointed to a spot on the map, "Here, which would be at ten o'clock from the point building, it's the largest building in the commune, and has a detached trailer right behind it. Our zoomies intel shows that the building is a place of worship with the Iman living in the trailer at its six." Zoomies were the drone operators who had done recon prior to the operation.

The plans were set. They would be going in as teams of two and taking out every adult they found. "The AF members are known for their weapons stockpiles and underground training facilities, so don't dismiss any opening as insignificant." He continued.

"Four buildings are facing Rolling Hill Road. Only one entrance off the road to the main compound, that's Sheikh Gilani Lane. That road branches off into several drives, each one with at least one building. We estimate ten trailers and four stationary buildings. Team 1-3, start the sweep at the trees and work your way in."

Vic looked around at the group meaningfully. "We don't want to risk getting Starbucks killed, so slay the oxygen thieves, snake eaters, silent mode. On my count, -10."

Everything was done in a well-coordinated fashion. Nadia was impressed. She hadn't seen anything like that since the early days in the CHEN, the Women's Corps of the Israel Defense Forces. Snake eaters, military slang for the US Army Special Forces, also known as the Green Berets. That explains their expertise. She could not wait to tell Eve that her code name for the mission was Starbucks.

The first thing Nadia did was take out the perimeter guards, two at the gate and six walking. She took them down quickly, using a knife, a favorite weapon of hers.

Two sets of men went out to the trailers and did a body count via the earpiece, five adults down, three kids tied up, duct-taped mouths shut. Nadia thought to herself, Seems a little harsh, but better than killing them.

In units consisting of two to three members, they made their way to the four stationary buildings. Nadia was teamed up with the tallest one in the group. She looked over at him, resting against a tree with a face of utter nonchalance as if he were merely waiting for a bus on a spring day. He had tousled red-brown hair and was wearing a short black jacket, black trousers, and ankle combat boots; he wore a dagger on his belt and exposed shoulder holsters, a bullet-proof vest offered extra padding over his muscular body. He caught her looking and smiling, smiling as if something good were about to happen. Nadia grinned back. She knew what he was feeling, an eagerness only those faced with death time and time again could understand.

When Nadia made it inside the building, she verified the space was a place of worship. Immediately inside, there was a second wall, with low wooden benches in front of the wall two feet off the ground. Under the benches were several pairs of shoes, including children's sizes. In addition to her two knives, she had two firearms, HK45 tactical pistols with silencers at the ready. They walked into what she assumed was the worship area. But what she found there was unexpected.

Men and women sleeping on the floors in sleeping bags. A quick headcount said twenty-five to thirty adults and six children. She knew this could get out of hand quickly if they did not handle it correctly. She checked the silencer and proceeded to walk up and down the aisles of sleeping people, shooting them in the head as she walked by. She left the children asleep. After the first row, she looked over at her partner, and yes, he was following her lead. In a matter of minutes, they were all dead, and none of the children woke. Nadia was grateful for that.

Over the earpiece, she got the news, "Team five lead, we found her, first assessment, likely bones were broken, several injury points, she's unconscious, but she's alive, Starbuck's alive."

Nadia was relieved. She knew that John would not be able to live with the news of his daughter's death. Nadia wasn't quite sure how she would've handled the loss. Over the headset, she asked the team five lead, "Location?"

"We're in building D, basement level. Send assistance."

"Roger, I'll be right there."

As she walked toward the exit, one of the kids woke up and looked at her. Nadia quickly assessed African American female, four to six years old. She was about to raise her gun but stopped herself and whispered to the little girl, "Honey, go back to sleep; everything's okay." The child laid back down, not knowing her mother and father lying next to her were both dead. The sun was just starting to rise when they finally brought Eve out into the light.

When Nadia saw her, she could not help but gasp. She couldn't believe somebody had done this to her friend, her family. Eve's mangled lip, injured face, and likely broken nose were caked in dried blood, congealed, and cracked. Her skin was colorless. It had taken on the pallor of a corpse. Blood slid down her leg and soaked the cloth material of her pants, merging with other wounds slowly flowing from her cuff, bright red and sticky in the daylight. There was an overwhelming stench of urine, metal, sweat, and fear. Nadia knew Eve hadn't gone down without a fight.

Coming up behind her was a woman crying. She turned around just in time to see two men flanking a seemingly tall, slender African American woman. The cut across her forehead dripped blood onto her once beautiful dress, now in shreds. Walking seemed to be a chore for her, but the men did not let this minor detail get in the way. Together, they dragged her across the ground to Vic. Unfortunately, her shoes were also missing. A headscarf was wrapped around her neck, with each man responsible for the ends, which they pulled tight, nearly strangling the stranger. Nadia felt no sympathy for her. She grew up in a world where women were just as violent as men. In fact, Nadia believed women were more dangerous, and she had little doubt that this woman was at fault, along with the men.

The woman was crying, repeating a name, Rafael, repeatedly. Vic asked her how they knew about Eve. The woman remained silent. He said, "I'll ask you one more time, if you don't answer me, I'll hand you over to them," indicating the group of men still high from the kills, splattered with blood, shuffling their feet like they were aching for more.

"How did you know about the woman?"

"Somebody called us, a man. He said Dr. Nicole Mathers was working undercover and that her real name was Special Agent Evelyn Black. That's all he said."

"I'm only going to ask you this once; who was it?"

The woman wailed, "I don't know, I don't know, he never said his name! He just said she wasn't Dr. Mathers." She broke down sobbing and barely audible, repeated the name 'Rafael, you killed my Rafael."

"Well, lady, if you have nothing else to tell me, I'm done with you too," Vic looked at the man on her right and nodded.

Before the man had a chance to fire his weapon,

Nadia walked up to her and said with a very calm and matter-of-fact tone, "My name is Nadia Katz. You nearly killed my friend. Prepare to die." She hoped someone got the movie reference. Nadia was a Princess Bride fan and had waited years to say that line. Then she stabbed the woman repeatedly, until she was dead.

Adrenaline was still shooting through Nadia's veins. She was just as high as the men. Bloodlust was something they had in common. Now she had to take care of her friend. She took one look at Eve and hoped that the broken person in front of her would survive this ordeal, both physically and mentally.

They placed Eve in the backseat of Vic's SUV, her head resting on Nadia's lap. Nadia continued to stroke the unconscious Eve's hair and frequently reminded her that she was with friends and safe. When she had Eve settled, and they were on the road, Nadia called John and let him know that Eve was with them, alive. She let him know Eve had some injuries but that they were taking her to get medical attention, and she would keep him posted.

Eve opened her eyes, looked up at Nadia, and in a weak voice, she managed to get out, "I knew you would find me. I need coffee."

Hearing Eve talk prompted Vic to turn around, look at the women and say, "How YOU doin'?"

Eve chuckled, winced in pain, and uttered, "That's not Jersey. It's Joey."

He guffawed, "I better work on that. My family are huge Friends fans. What can I say?" And then he held up a thermos and said, "*Starbucks* Sumatra, just how you like it." Then he produced a straw and said, "I thought you might need this."

Vic made a phone call to the police, let them know what they would find at the AF compound, and then tossed the phone out the window. They drove for a few hours and both Eve and Nadia slept. The next thing Nadia knew, they were in the garage of a friend of Vic's, a physician friend.

The doctor, the driver, and Vic got Eve into this house's makeshift examining/surgery room. Once Eve was settled, the doctor kicked them out of the room. Vic went into the kitchen to make some coffee, and Nadia fell asleep on the sofa.

When Eve awoke several hours later, a little high from the pain medicine, she called her dad and told him she was okay. Her voice was slurred from the medicine and missing teeth. Vic assured her that a dentist would be available when she was ready. Man, he thought of everything.

She then called Franklin. She had not spoken to him in several days, and she felt the need to let him know all was fine. He was her husband, after all.

When he answered the phone and realized Eve was on the line, he sounded surprised, "Hey baby, I wondered what you've been doing. I haven't heard from you. I tried to call you back last night, but you didn't answer the phone; and whose phone is this anyway? I don't recognize the number."

Oh yeah, that's why he was surprised, "It's Nadia's

phone. My phone quit working. I'm not sure how busy house and all, but no one 'fessed up. I must get a new one soon. Other than that, everything's good; having a wonderful time with the family, and I may stay a couple days longer than planned if that works for you."

"Sure thing, love. I'm glad you're having a good time with your family. I'll see you soon."

This time, she wouldn't forget to say, "I love you, Franklin."

"Oh baby, I love you too. Come home soon. I miss my family." They hung up, and Eve felt much better.

Unknown to Vic, his team, and the al-Fuqura members, an unwelcome stranger was in the compound, watching and listening. Sure, there are more powerful binoculars, but nothing is better. The Vortex Optics Kaibab HD binoculars were top of the line and easy to purchase quickly without a paper trail.

No one ever looks up. Threats to humans rarely come from above, so sitting up in a tree at the AF Compound, just thirty feet from the action, was as safe as sitting on top of a hill fifty miles away. The only difference was that at this distance, voices were easily distinguished. Had there been any severe danger to Eve, a phone call would have been made to the police. Who knew they had underground torture rooms? Perhaps the risk to Eve had been miscalculated. Her friends had undoubtedly saved the day, no surprise. This trip had been maybe the cheapest but most enjoyable so far. There would surely be more to come before Eve would give up. She just needed time to lick her wounds, and then she would continue to search for the person behind the photos.

Chapter Seven

Recovery at Tres Piedras

The trek back to Tres Piedras and her children was made more tolerable by Vic's ability to convince a colleague, Ms. Jacqueline Mars, the candy heiress, to lend him her corporate jet. Eve would never underestimate her friend again.

They arrived fifteen minutes before takeoff and boarded straight from their car. There was no baggage weigh-in or X-raying of bags. There was zero waiting on the tarmac. As soon as they boarded, the crew closed the aircraft door and took off.

The staff aboard the plane did all they could to make Eve as comfortable as possible. They may not have known what had happened, but just one look at her, the bruised face, black eyes, and dislocated nose, along with the cane, let them know she needed some personal assistance.

If asked, Eve's plan was to tell people that she was in a car accident. She did not expect to see anyone over the next couple of days, and by then, according to her doctor, the swelling would fade, but not the black eyes. They usually disappear within one to two weeks. The dark blue-violet color should gradually fade after a few days to a yellowish-green. Thanks to her FBI fashion coach, Eve was adept at makeup. With a few YouTube videos, her skills in covering markings of abuse should improve. She will have plenty of time "resting" to practice.

With help, Eve managed to get into one of the cushy, soft, butter-like, ivory leather recliners. She was even more comfortable when the flight attendant showed her the deep-recline seat options. She rested with an ice pack covering her face while Nadia took a shower, and their two guards, gifts from Vic, played cards.

Who knew that even the air would smell better on a private jet? It smelled fresh, like clean linens, on a beach. The pillows and blanket were the softest Eve had ever experienced. She was in heaven, and for just a split second Eve thought the torture was almost worth it. She wanted to stay awake and enjoy the comfort of flying privately.

The flight attendant handed Eve a menu with a smile on her face, she let her know her options and whispered to Eve so no one else could hear, "You can have as much as you wish." At this, Eve knew she would never be content flying commercial.

Eve looked at the menu options. The list was long: The first course included Goat Cheese Truffles, Organic Mixed Greens, Walnuts, with a Vinaigrette Dressing, or the Petrossian Classic Ossetra caviar with Blinis, Sour Cream, Chopped Egg Whites, Red Onions, and Chives. The next course was a Wild Mushroom Veloute soup. The entrée choices included: a BLT Smoked Bacon, Beefsteak Tomato, Lettuce, Garlic Aioli, Grilled Sirloin Steak, Horseradish Cream, Onion, Tomato, a Maine Smoked Salmon, Dill Cream, Cucumber, and Tomato or the Poached Maine Lobster, Green Beans, Fingerling Potatoes, Tomatoes, Roasted Bell Peppers, Lemon Dill Dressing. For dessert, her choices were: Cantaloupe or Homemade Ice Cream served with Pineapple, Grapes, Strawberries, Dried Fruits, Walnuts, Marcona almonds, and Cashews.

Eve wanted it all, but she knew her limits. She looked up at the flight attendant and said with deep sorrow, "The soup and ice cream, please." There was no way she could eat anything solid with her jacked up mouth and likely broken nose. The attendant promised to bring her as much soup and plain ice cream as Eve could handle, and with that, she felt slightly better. Nadia had the truffles and mixed greens salad.

When they arrived at the Taos airport, the guards helped her off the plane and into an SUV nearly as comfortable as the plane. The driver took Eve, Nadia, and the guards to her father's home, helped her inside, and then the guards and driver left them.

After Eve was again settled, her father broke the news about Jim. He explained that Jim had been electrocuted while performing and was in serious condition in the hospital. Eve attempted to get up off the sofa upon hearing this, but that proved difficult, and she fell back against the cushions. She was on bed rest, which meant she wasn't getting off the sofa for at least two days, or so that's what her father told her.

Dr. Marconi, the village doctor, arrived at the house shortly after that and did a careful examination of Eve. Her nose was not broken, just severely bruised. It would heal straight. She had several cracked ribs and a torn meniscus, along with several cuts and bruises all over her body. The doctor explained to John that Eve might expect to experience panic attacks, depression, and PTSD. This is because waterboarding and physical torture had lasting effects on the mind and the body. However, with Eve's training and personal experiences, John and Nadia were sure the only wounds they needed to worry about with Eve were the physical ones. They knew she was not going to be an easy patient.

They were correct, Eve was not a very good patient, but for them, she had to try, "Nadia, can you get my laptop for me?"

"Sure," and she left the room and returned quickly with Eve's laptop and handed it to her.

When Eve opened the computer, she went straight to her email. Her fears were confirmed. There was another email waiting for her with two pictures attached and no content in the body of the email. The pictures included Jim and Eve sitting at the table at the club and then him alone on stage at the time of the electrocution. The sight was horrifying.

Because Jim survived and could likely identify the man, Eve was convinced that the person would return to finish the job. Jim was at the hospital, vulnerable, with no one there guarding him. Everyone assumed the electrocution was a freak accident, and why wouldn't they? She would have to revisit Seattle and talk to Jim, if that was possible, to see if he remembered seeing anyone suspicious.

Eve could not come to terms with the onslaught of emotions she was feeling. She wanted to get up off the sofa, put on her clothes, and go to Jim. This need was not out of love or loyalty; she knew that this was done because of her.

She recognized that getting up off the sofa was not feasible, let alone getting on a plane. She needed to heal, so instead, she begged for a cup of coffee from Mari, who then surprised her with a salted caramel protein milkshake.

John got his own cup of coffee and sat down on the chair next to Eve. "This is what I found out. Your agency has a classified white paper on how to hack the Nissan Leaf and other vehicles, so my guess is the killer is familiar with computers. Maybe not as good as me, but he has skills."

"Wait a minute, dad. Step back. Did you just tell me you hacked FBI files, classified ones?"

"Well, of course. They don't call me BobD world's greatest hacker for nothing."

"Oh, Dad, who called you the world's greatest hacker?"
"My dark web hacker friends, of course."

"Okay, okay, if you say so, Mr. BobD." Eve laughed, and the pain in her ribs made her groan.

Nadia, sitting on the ottoman, grabbed a sofa pillow and threw it at him, he dodged the pillow and laughed, but she nailed him with a second one. Eve watched them and thought how lucky she was to be part of a family that could laugh while in the midst of danger and death.

"What about the photos, John? Did you find out anything about them?" Nadia asked.

"The images lacked EXIF data, so I used an Air Force prototype to look at sensor noise." The looks on their faces said it all. He was speaking a foreign language. He gave an analogy they would understand, "It's like firing a handgun. All bullets have unique marks formed from the weapon's firing, like fingerprints. The sensor noise from the images sent to you in the envelope at your home and the sensor noise on the images in the email with Campbell, and we'll check the images of your friend Jim. Still, I'm pretty sure they will all turn out to be from the same camera."

He looked once again at their faces; good, still with me, he had not lost them. He continued, "I read that some camera manufacturers have a hidden watermark in their images, and I'm still checking that. However, it's my belief the sensor noise is conclusive data.

With this attempted murder, we'll assume that whoever sent you those photos will probably kill anyone you come into contact with."

Mari chimed in, "We know he's not going to be killing Elaine and Rafael." Crickets. Mari was concerned she had offended them. "Too early to make jokes like that?" She looked at them and could tell they were trying to conceal smiles.

Eve ignored the joke and continued the train of thought, "You guys are correct. We need to write down what we know about the killer.

Thanks to the call to the al-Fuqura cell, we know that he is male.

He's targeting more than people from the conference

There was a significant age difference between Jim and Campbell. And while Campbell was flirty, Jim was not, so we can't assume it's somebody obsessed with me.

Both of the events happened in the Northeast; maybe that's something?"

At that moment, Franklin's 2-month-old cries could be heard all over the house, and Harper decided she wanted to play with her mommy. So John helped his granddaughter up onto the sofa, with instructions to be very careful because mommy was not well, she snuggled up close, and the two lay together while Mari read them a story. Soon mommy and daughter were both fast asleep, and that was pretty much how they spent the remainder of the afternoon and evening.

The next day, earlier than recommended, Eve was able to walk with the assistance of a cane. So it came as a shock to them all when she said she was going to visit Karl, her friend from the 6th grade. Apparently, his mother was still in contact with many of the villagers. It took John very little time to retrieve Karl's address.

"Eve, the only way you are stepping foot out of this house is if you take Nadia with you!"

Eve knew she needed someone to drive, but she did not need a bodyguard. She was not helpless. One look at her dad and Nadia, knowing there was no reason to argue. She wouldn't win. After breakfast, they drove to his place. Eve hoped the spontaneity of her decision and not telling anyone outside the immediate household would keep Karl safe.

When they arrived at his house, Eve's first thought she expressed aloud to Nadia was that the place looked more fitting for someone her father's age, not a young person like Karl.

Then she thought, who am I kidding? Karl probably lives with his mom. She imagined him as an overweight gamer, spending his time alone and in the basement of his mother's house, both living off her Social Security checks. Considering his mom's size back in the day, Eve doubted that Karl's mom was all that healthy.

As she prepared to go up to the door, Eve realized what a hypocrite she was. She was immediately offended when anybody looked at her and judged her based on her appearance. She remembered a maid in a hotel once called her fat and how she got even by breaking her nose. Eve was characterizing Karl the same way. So what if he carries a few pounds, he was a friendly kid, and probably a nice man! She admonished herself.

You could imagine her surprise when the door was opened by a very attractive man with an athletic build, dressed in a pair of worn Gore-Tex trousers, a white tee, and comfortable-looking hiking boots. His hair was thick and blonde, and his eyes were a blend of green and blue. This was not the pudgy sixth-grader, afraid of heights, the boy who would do anything for a kiss from 12-year-old Eve.

"Karl?"

He answered with a slight hesitation, "Yes, who are you two?"

"It's Eve, Evie Black. We were neighbors at the SFH compound."

"I remember you," he gave her the once over, something she felt was inappropriate. It made her uncomfortable, "Wow, you've grown, but you look like shit. Sorry, I should not have said that. What happened to you?"

"A car accident. It's no big deal."

Karl noticed the exotic beauty next to Eve, and his concern for Eve and her obvious pain disappeared, "Who's your friend?"

Nadia gave him a look of disgust, "Men, they are nothing more than big boys." Eve could have sworn that Nadia's accent got really thick when she said that.

"She is my good friend, Nadia." She almost told him about her relationship with John but held back, "Did you know Camilla died a few years ago?"

"Yes, I heard about that. I'm sorry I couldn't make it to the funeral; I was in Tanzania climbing Mount Kilimanjaro and couldn't make it back. Mother was there. She commented on how good Camilla looked, peaceful and happy. Everybody loved her, and boy was she a good cook." He patted his stomach and said, "I was lucky that we moved away so I could shed some of those extra pounds I had as a kid. I can't say that would have been easy had I been close enough to enjoy her cooking. I would still be that chubby little boy you remember so..." He raised his eyebrows and gave her a hopeful look, "fondly?"

Nadia looked him over. She found it hard to believe this man was ever pudgy. He was handsome but not her type. She liked older men. They understood her. Maybe there was a little bit of "finding her daddy" in her choice of men, but she was okay with that.

"Where are my manners? Do you two want to come in?"

When they walked into the house, the smell of baked goods and cleaning products overwhelmed her senses. The walls had a faded wallpaper with, she squinted her eyes to get a better look, peacocks, yep, peacocks with colors that would have overwhelmed the room years ago. Now it just lent itself to a flower garden feel. The look of the living room was predictable. It had a chintz couch, two matching chairs, both with doilies across the top and on the arms, and a coffee table in the center. The sofa was a rose-pink color and made Eve want to curl up and take a nap. The coffee table was topped with glass and supported by painted white wood legs. House. A United States map was spread out on the low table, with handwritten notes in the margins. A gold shag carpet that she knew had to be from the 1970s was also faded but would feel delicious to walk on with bare feet. The papered walls, and the matching furniture, all contributed to the room's comfortable grandmother-like charm. An attached dining room with a china cabinet and a highly polished table with a faux flower centerpiece completed the look.

Eve was less interested in the décor and more in the baked goods smell, causing her stomach to growl. She hoped they would be offered something to eat before they began the difficult conversation.

After painful hugs, hellos, and small talk, they made their way into the kitchen, where a kettle was on, and fresh cookies were cooling on the counter. On the way to the kitchen, they passed through a narrow hall loaded with photos of pudgy Karl as a boy and of him with his mother. As they progressed down the hall, the photos progressed as well. There were photos of slim Karl on top of mountains. The pictures were good for a glance as you worked your way toward the kitchen but were not interesting enough to invite closer examination.

Once you arrived in the kitchen, the floor no longer had carpet. Instead, it had linoleum with a gold and white floral pattern. There was a giant oak table in the middle of the floor, nearly as big as the one at John's house. This was the room where the entertaining happened. The walls were white and decorated with collector's plates and a wall clock that ticked and tocked so loudly that Eve was sure she would have destroyed it had she been in one of her pre-coffee moods. The cupboards were old, but clean, and the window over the sink had white shutters.

Although the house wasn't large, the house was full of love. Growing up here, away from the desert, she believed that growing up here must have been warm and cozy.

As they made their way into the kitchen, Eve felt obligated to ask Karl about his mother's health.

"She's not doing well. I lived in Colorado until last year, when she was diagnosed with terminal cancer, so I came back home to take care of her. She's upstairs resting."

Wow, what a good son, Eve thought. At least he did not pick a profession that caused him and his mom to be estranged for several years. She was proud of herself; she had guessed right about the house belonging to his mother. She was happy that she was wrong about him being a lazy gamer mooching off her. Carl made them both a cup of tea. Nadia with two sugars, and Eve had none. She hoped the tea was not Earl Grey. Earl Grey was black tea flavored with oil from the bergamot orange and upset her stomach.

Before she took a sip, she knew this would be enjoyable. The scent was familiar, cinnamon spice, followed by cardamom, basil, clove, and orange. She inhaled deeply and took a drink. The tea was naturally sweet, just how Eve liked it. This was pretty much a number two on the scale of drink preferences.

She sat back in the chair, talked with Karl about college, joined the FBI, and then told him about her marriage and her two kids. She almost forgot to mention those small details. Nadia was walking about, exploring, looking for anything that could say he was their guy.

Eve decided to go upstairs and say hello to Mrs. P., not because she wanted to see her, but because she felt obligated. After all, Eve was blamed for Mrs. P.'s son's broken leg in the sixth grade. Eve walked up the stairs and thought the creaking stairs would undoubtedly prevent any secret late-night trips to the kitchen. She crept down the short hall, passing a glossy pink bathroom dead-ended at his mother's main bedroom entrance.

The hardwood floor had a large area rug, recently vacuumed, with a flower design and fringe. The room was clean, yet had the odor of old people, mildly sweet and musty. The only light came from the windows. Warm yellow sun rays wafted through the glass, and dust motes floated about, suspended in the air, aged, sheer curtains bloused on the floor.

As she crept closer to Mrs. P.'s bed, Eve tried not to gag on the aroma of sweat and sickness. What she saw reminded her of Camila in the hospital, a woman near death. Once a plump, sweet, to be honest, that's not true, Mrs. P. was a not-so-sweet, woman, now barely a hundred pounds, and on a respirator. The aged lady looked like she would not make it another week. A woman was on a chair across from the bed, presumably a nurse. She sat there without making a sound and startled Eve when she noticed her.

"Hello," she greeted the nurse, "Is Mrs. P. awake?"

"No, she hasn't been conscious for a few days now. Things are not looking good. She should be at the hospital, but she insisted that she wanted to die at home, and Karl, such a loving son, is doing all he can to make her last days comfortable. He's a good boy."

Well, that was an overshare, but she appreciated the background, and of course, it confirmed her belief that

Karl was perhaps the catch that got away. So, as Eve and Nadia prepared to leave, she gave Karl a hug and a quick kiss on the lips and said, "I owed you that one."

He tightened the hug, causing Eve to wince in pain, and told her not to be a stranger.

The two got in the car and drove the twenty miles northwest, back to Tres Piedras

A few minutes into the drive, Nadia said to Eve, "I think we can cross that name off the list. If things don't work out between you and Franklin, you might want to check back up with that guy."

"I don't think so."

They drove the rest of the way with no conversation, John Coltrane playing on the stereo.

Chapter Eight

SeaTac

When Eve recovered enough to get on a plane and head back to Seattle, she did so, and upon arrival, she took an Uber directly to the hospital. After playing good patient for what felt like forever, the freedom she felt getting away left her feeling light and cheery, even if the destination was unfavorable.

Eve had spent much of the last two days repeatedly hitting refresh on her email. She was worried that more photos would show up, and they would be of Karl, dead. She didn't know if they would be at his mother's or a staged mountain climbing accident. This person, this killer, was certainly fond of making his prey appear to be victims of accidents rather than of murder. To date, there had been no new emails, and the pictures were just those of Campbell and Jim, nothing of al-Fuqura nor of Karl. She should learn to count her blessings.

Eve needed directions to Jim's room. The patient rooms looked the same, with glass walls and curtains closed, concealing the people inside. The doors were a dark brown-black, and the nameplates were the only items giving clues to the identity of the occupants. With almost a sense of pride, the nurse announced, "We're here." She smiled and opened the door wide. Doctors and nurses surrounded his hospital bed, attaching IV's, heart monitors, and oxygen tanks. When the nurse saw all the activity happening inside, she suggested Eve wait down the hall, in the ICU waiting room.

As Eve entered the large open visitors' space, she was greeted with a welcoming smile from a receptionist who invited her to have a cup of coffee or something from the vending machine. The room itself was impressive but not elegant, with assorted chairs. Some were oversized and comfortable. Others were upright with padding, all in complementary brown, ivory, and sea blue, green easy-to-clean faux leather. Magazines in plastic sleeves were neatly arranged on an enormous central cherry wood table. Watercolor artwork on the walls made the space feel less like a hospital, as did the neutral tan walls and the play corner for young children.

She stared at the wall in front of her, trying to review her notes in her mind in an attempt to forget she was in a hospital. Eve was uncomfortable in the waiting room and chose not to eat because of the risk of exposure to surface contaminants. Several others were in the room with her, but the space was tranquil. She scanned the room, selected a chair that looked particularly clean, and sat down, gingerly. The drive had taken a toll on her. Eve was not yet recovered enough to make this trip without feeling like she should be in a hospital room herself.

A man was sitting near Eve. She saw him as a brownish blur on her right and was only made aware of him because of his constant movements. Eve picked up a magazine and started flipping through the pages. Then, with an exaggerated turn of her head, she was able to get a better look at him. He was wearing a brown waterproof overcoat, a little too big for him, and a matching fedora. His eyes spoke of deep pain, and the evidence of tears was still plain on his face. The man's body was hunched forward, and despite having never met him before, she knew she was looking at pure grief. His hands were aged and had a slight tremor. They rested on what looked to be a well-read book. He felt her staring in his direction and looked over at her. Eve offered a smile and then quickly looked away. She did not want to get caught up in someone else's emotions.

On the other side of the L-shaped room, she could hear arguing, the dropping of items in a vending machine, and the pop and fizz of a soda can being opened. Sitting too long left her, massaging her neck and shoulders, crossing and re-crossing her legs, and shaking herself to stay awake. Eve decided to get a cup of coffee after all.

When she was finally allowed to go into Jim's room, she stood against the wall while several people still crowded around him. An old TV was hanging from the ceiling, with a game show on mute. A window brought in plenty of light and shone brightly on the flowers and plants, giving an illusion of a happy place. In the end, Eve was looking at a typical hospital room, sparse and functional. Its walls were a warm cream color and acted as a backdrop for artwork, attached by tape and clearly made by children for the man in the bed. The room had an undertone of bleach and the aseptic odor of carbolic acid masked by the distracting smell of the flowers.

Among all the hospital staff, a middle-aged woman who could only be Jim's mother was in the room. Martha, a widow from Iowa, looked just as Eve would have expected, a floral print dress, sensible shoes, and the obligatory short hairstyle, a popular trend for ladies over sixty. Yet, despite her age, her eyes sparkled and were as blue as Jim's. Eve introduced herself, "I knew Jim in college. I'm Eve, Eve Black." The woman immediately embraced her, crushing her already bruised ribs. She was incredibly uncomfortable, physically and mentally.

"Eve! I've wanted to meet you for so many years to thank you. Jim spoke so highly of you." Her voice was choked with emotion. "Everything you did for my Jimmy..." Her voice tapered off, and her eyes started to water. Clearly, Martha did not know her son was in the hospital because of Eve, and she hoped his mother would never find out.

Earlier that morning, he had gone into cardiac arrest due to the heart's electrical effect. His heart had stopped, and now Jim's doctors had him in a medically induced coma due to pain. They could do magic for most pain, but nerve pain was something that could drive a person to suicide. He was also wrapped up from head to toe, with his left arm and leg the exception.

"Ma'am, do you mind if I sit here for a while?"

"No, honey, you go right ahead. I was just ready to go to the cafeteria and get a bit of lunch and a cup of coffee. Can I bring you back anything?"

Eve wanted to say yes, rarely did she turn down coffee, and her stomach growled at the mere idea of food, but she told the woman, "No, thank you."

Eve appreciated that his mom gave her time to be alone with Jim. She wanted to ask a doctor, nurse, or anyone in white, about his prognosis. Would he survive? Would he be permanently scarred? Would he be forced to give up his career in music? This was all too much for Eve.

The bandages were on the right side of his body, so she believed holding his left hand would be fine. Instead, she leaned down and spoke to him, "I will find out who did this to you, and I will get them."

Eve did not hear Wendy, Jim's wife, walk into the room, so she was unaware that her words to Jim were overheard, "What do you mean, who did this to him? This was an accident."

Eve was immediately startled by the intrusion and had to think fast. She turned around and immediately recognized Wendy, the woman in the green dress from so many years ago. She walked over and took the woman's hand.

"Hello Wendy, it's so good to see you again. I'm Eve Black. You may remember me from Columbia. I'm now Special Agent Eve Black, and I guess my profession makes me jump to conclusions. You're right, of course. No one was to blame for the accident, electrocution, so I'm told, and I'm really sorry." Eve glanced down at her watch, "I really must be getting back. I have a husband and my children to get to, they need me. I just wanted to come up here and tell you how sad I am about this happening to such a good man."

Wendy nodded her head in agreement, "Yes, Jim is a good man," She gave Eve a brief hug, "And of course, I remember you. You set us up. Jim told me you wrote a note with my phone number and name and told him to find me, said I was perfect for him, his soul mate. You were right, and now I think I'm going to lose him, and his children will be without their daddy."

Wendy broke down crying and leaned into her. Eve wanted to get the hell out of there, but how could she do that now with this woman crying and clearly out of control. At that moment, Jim's mother returned and saved the day. Wendy embraced her mother-in-law, and they both cried together. Eve slipped out of the room.

Before leaving the hospital, she decided to call in a few favors. Eve had a couple of FBI friends at the Seattle field office, and they owed her. She would persuade them to keep an eye on Jim without her office ever finding out. So she made a call to FBI Special Agent Cathy Baker. "Hey Cathy, it's been a long time. It's Eve Black."

"Hi Eve, how are things in Alabama?"

"Pretty slow; however, I am on this undercover case, and I need your help. First, it's got to be off-the-record. Do you think you could do that? Second, I would like both you and Mav to step up if you can. The victim is a good man, and he was electrocuted by a person that did it simply to get my attention. It's related to that undercover job at an arms conference I did a few years ago.

"The terrorist convention in Cincinnati?" "Yes."

"I remember that job. Those New York days were fun, weren't they? It's really too bad you guys were sent to Alabama and Mav and I to Seattle. You get the sunshine and the rain, and we also have wonderful coffee! If I remember correctly, you don't have blood in your veins. Instead, you have dark roasted Sumatra."

Eve admitted, "Yes, my coffee habit is still strong, but enough small talk. Unfortunately, I have to get back and won't be able to check on him, so if you think you and Mav could do this for me for the next week or so, I'd really appreciate it, and I'll owe you both."

"You know we're here for you. Just email me the details: the room number, hospital, and his family. We'll make sure somebody is always there keeping an eye on him."

"If you need to hire a few security people, it's on my dime. I'll work out the details with my office when the mission's over."

"No worries, I have a few friends that owe me favors. Mav and I will take care of your guy. You go do what you have to do to catch the person that did this."

"Thank you, Cathy. I appreciate it. Maybe you and Mav could take a vacation and visit us in Alabama." Eve knew they would never come, so she was comfortable inviting them.

"Sure, let's do that someday," Cathy spoke, for that will never happen, but not because we don't love you; it's because we can't stand your husband, your arrogant, thinks he's better than everybody else, husband. The last time the four of them were together, Mav almost punched Franklin.

Eve took an Uber back to the airport and was on the next plane back to Taos, back to her father's house. Meanwhile, dressed in scrubs and holding an old clipboard found at the nurses' station, the uninvited guest drew no attention as he watched people go in and out of Jim's room. He was surprised to see Eve. That was unpredictable. She was back in the game earlier than expected after the al-Fuqura fiasco. She hadn't stayed very long. Interesting...

When FBI Special Agent Cathy Baker showed up, he knew his plans would have to change just an hour after Eve left. He looked down the hall. Agent Baker wasn't sitting outside Jim's door, nor did she introduce herself to his family. Still, she was just inside the visitor's area, ten feet from his room. He knew why Eve was there, but told himself this was not a big deal. Jim wasn't going anywhere, and she could not be there 24/7.

He looked down at his watch when another agent showed up, nearly midnight. This was turning into a long night. The two talked for a short time. When the female left, her replacement settled in her place with a coffee. He glanced up and down the hall, adjusted his gun, and leaned back in the chair. Looks like he was going to be there for several hours. So tonight, Jim would live, but tomorrow was another day.

He returned to the hospital the following day and found the laundry service in the basement of the building. When no one was around, he sought out the cleanest-looking forest green scrubs he could find. That was the color that the patient care techs wore at this hospital. He already had a Photo-shopped badge he had created the night before and carried his trusty clipboard. It's incredible how something like a clipboard could make you look like you belong.

When he got to Jim's floor, he did not see either of the agents or anyone inside the room. Instead, a quick scan of the space revealed a web of cords entering and exiting, beeping monitors and other pieces of equipment signifying the patient was still alive. Most were unfamiliar to him, but he had done his homework and quickly identified the respirator. A deep, resonant voice from behind barked as he reached down to unplug it. "What the hell are you doing?"

Without hesitation, he reached into his boxers, under his scrubs, and pulled out a syringe containing Succinylcholine, a short-term paralytic. He had learned this trick when doing his own type of deep dive on Eve. He was prepared for anything. He raised his voice a bit and gave it a feminine flair to provide the stranger with a sense that he was not dangerous and walked up to the man, all the while hiding the syringe behind his back and reaching out with the other as if to shake hands, "Hi, I'm David. We haven't met. I'm the PCT, the patient care tech. I was checking to make sure that everything was running just fine." When he got close enough to the man, he plunged the syringe into his neck with one hand, held the man up with the other, and then dragged him to the nearest chair.

He left the hospital without completing the mission. The job was too hot. His only recourse was to finish it when Jim was back in Iowa.

When the paralytic effects of the medicine wore off and the security guard could move again, the first thing he did was call Agent Baker to let her know what happened. Cathy was relieved that the guard she hired survived the encounter, keeping things uncomplicated. But unfortunately, it meant this incident would not have reached her superiors. So instead, she called and briefed Eve. "It's just my opinion, Eve, but I think the man will not return in all likelihood. The room's bustling, and he now knows people are guarding your patient, so I don't think he'll be returning."

Chapter Nine

Back to NYC

Eve had not been back to New York City in more than two years. Just being at *La Guardia* felt like home. She stopped at *Whole Bean* for a cup of coffee and smiled as she passed *Hudson News, Afaze,* and *Brookstone,* remembering her last time here. The flight back to Taos was uneventful; she had a Bloody Mary and read The American Terrorist. Unfortunately, there was a lady in the seat adjacent to hers and no one in the window seat. Before Eve had a chance to fret over the invasion of her personal space, the middle-seat lady moved to the window, putting a seat between them. The pretzels were stale, the air was stale, and she yearned for the luxury she had experienced on her last flight.

She called an Uber and waited by the automated glass doors near the baggage claim. The driver showed up in less than ten minutes, and as soon as she sat down, he attacked her. Or at least that was how it felt to Eve. He immediately offered her candy, started showing her photos of his children, and suggested she link her iPhone so she could choose the music. Behind the passenger seat, he had a plastic multi-item holder, like the kind you would find on hooks in closets or hanging behind doors. Instead of shoes or socks, these little plastic pockets held combs, floss, mints, business cards for fun places in the city, and much more. The whole thing was essentially an over-the-seat Uber concierge.

She really just wanted the driver to stop talking to her, so she made a show of placing a call and spoke loudly into the phone to her father. They were all a little on edge. Both she and her dad were now convinced it must be Payton of the New York four; however, Nadia was not convinced. Eve let them know her plans, and even after they hung up, she kept the phone to her ear and pretended she was still in conversation. She knew the driver wasn't fooled, but as long as he shut up, Eve didn't care.

Eve remembered from the interview three years ago that Payton was an electrician. He was the only one of the New York four terror cell who was not in prison, incarcerated for a bombing and murder she was responsible for. As an electrician, he could have gotten the specs for the Nissan Leaf to figure out the hack or set up the microphone to electrocute Jim. He would know enough about the hospital equipment to understand what could be messed with to best kill a patient.

Eve was convinced Payton was her man and his motivation for killing her friends was pure revenge. If she was correct, he was going to regret it. And if she was wrong and Payton became a target as well, she would know the person was not just targeting the Northwest.

Karl was still alive and well. She had been texting him under the pretense of checking up on his mother. He asked her to go out to dinner with him when Eve returned. She reminded him that she was a married woman. Instead of giving up, he asked if her girlfriend, the beautiful Israeli, would be available. At that point, she let him know Nadia was dating her father. His mind was blown.

All the flights were draining her savings. It's not like she could use the shared account, or ask the mother-in-law. The thought of interacting with Franklin's mother by choice made her shudder. Her father did find some good deals, but not good enough, and flying on standby was not an option. John never had more than twenty-four hours to buy her ticket, so how good of a deal could he get? At this rate, she would use up all her savings. But her frequent flyer miles should be scoring her some great seats. At least this trip sent her to her favorite spot, New York, and then to a small town just a few miles north of the city.

It took some digging, but her dad finally got an address. He said something about a lottery and speaking to a grandma. Eve really didn't care. She just wanted to know where to go.

When Eve showed up at his home, Payton was the one to open the door, and when he saw her, he slammed it shut. She knocked again, this time a little harder, and when he opened it again, he asked, "What do you want? Why are you here?"

"Payton, it's me, Dr. Mathers."

"Yes, I know who you are. You are the woman that set us up, that sent my friends to jail for a crime they did not commit. I don't know how you did it or why you did it, but I know you are to blame, Jackson, told me about the sunglasses."

After a night of fun with Jackson at the conference, she took his sunglasses, promising to return them when they next met. She then left those same sunglasses on his dresser in the hotel room the morning of the explosion.

Eve didn't know why she left the sunglasses in his room, thus giving Jackson a clue that she was behind the arrest.

Her only excuse was that she wasn't thinking straight, and yes, he was right; she set them up, and she did frame two of them for the explosion and murder of the security guards. But seriously! The New York Four were not fine upstanding citizens. Not long ago, they claimed entrapment and got off for a crime they clearly had full intentions of committing.

Eve had been careful not to frame Payton or Jackson, but somehow Jackson was convicted, and she had no idea why. But, of course, Eve wasn't going to explain all of this to Payton.

"Payton, I understand your frustration, your anger, but I'm not responsible. Yes, I left the sunglasses when I stopped by to see Jackson. We were going to spend some time together. I believe someone hacked my phone. They read my text messages and listened to my phone calls. I was there waiting for you guys to show up, decided to get a coffee at *Starbucks*, and heard an explosion. The police led your friends out in handcuffs when I returned to your hotel. I got nervous and ran."

She continued, "Payton, someone is killing my friends."

Payton looked at her face. It looked sincere. She looked troubled and sad. Incredulously, he believed her. He made a quick judgment that maybe Dr. Mathers wasn't the one that set them up.

Payton welcomed her into his home and introduced her to his wife and two of his three daughters, the other already off at college. Then, Payton suggested the two go for a walk so they could talk in private.

Eve had a plan. She would share with Payton everything she knew and carefully watch his behavior. She would pay attention to the non-verbals that would call him out as guilty: significant pauses in the responses, the changes in facial expression, the looks of anger, nervousness, hesitation, confusion, and concern.

As they walked down the street, Eve shared with Payton what she knew about the death of Campbell, and the electrocution of Jim, both men she had spent time with over the past week. He looked at her, brows drawn close, face tightening, and pressed lips made it clear his idea of 'spending time' was not the same as hers.

"I meant I spent time with them talking, having dinner, not sexual. I'm married and have two children of my own." She knew what to say to win the trust of others.

It worked. While Payton knew many women who would happily cheat on their husbands, he could tell by how she looked so insulted at the mere idea she was cheating that Nicole was a decent and faithful woman.

As she spoke to Payton, she continued to take note of his reactions. Eve believed he was the most likely candidate before the walk, but now she had her doubts. Because he was her top suspect, Eve had not taken any chances and had a car following them.

Vic's friend was behind the steering wheel of a nondescript car, maintaining visuals and moving at a pace equal to their walking. Nevertheless, he was ready to pounce if Payton became aggressive.

The walking was hard for Eve. She should have brought her cane, but she had left it behind. They were quite the sight walking down the street together. Payton, now an Iman, wearing flowing robes and a beard, looking quite devout, and Eve with her worn jeans and a graphic X-Men t-shirt. She was looking very casual, very American.

With minimal prodding, Payton told Eve that he spoke with Jackson often. Still, his relationship with Jim and Bill, the other NY4 cell members, had deteriorated. He told her of Jackson's location if Dr. Mathers wanted to reach out and mend the relationship. He was at a minimum-security prison in Lebanon, Ohio, and was set to be released in five years. Apparently, the absence of incriminating evidence in Payton's room kept him free of an indictment. The same had not proven true for Jackson. Eve thought it would work for them both. She had only intended to frame the other two.

What can you do? The judicial system is fickle.

Eve was more confused than ever. She had been so convinced Payton was the one, but she knew instinctively that he was innocent after speaking with him.

She had no idea who was doing this to her, and she was exhausted. This was one of those days where tiredness comes in physical and mental forms. Her body needed to sleep, but her mind needed to keep going, to burn the stress she was feeling right out. How many days had it been since she worked out? Without exercise, her mind would keep her awake. She needed distractions that did not exacerbate the problem.

They made it back to Payton's house, and she thanked him for talking with her. Once she was out of sight of Payton's home, she slumped exhausted into the car that had been tailing them.

The driver took her back to the hotel. As she carried her weary and injured self down the hall and up the elevator, then down two more halls to her room. Eve remembered she did not have her key.

Bloody hell, Eve just leaned against the door and slid to the floor. She sighed, pulled out her phone, called her dad, and shared the meeting outcome with Payton. After ending the call, Eve leaned her head against the wall, and a full five minutes passed before she rose to her feet and made her way back to the front desk for a new key card from an oddly nervous desk clerk.

Once inside her room, she noticed immediately that something was wrong. Could this be why the clerk was looking so nervous? Then she spotted the reason, and it came in a box. It took her a few minutes to recognize the smell, but when she did, she smiled. A pizza box from Grimaldi's was on her bed, the best pizza pie in Brooklyn, and a screw-top bottle of Moscato wine. The attached note said, Get some rest, Vic.

Eve sighed with relief, her fatigue disappearing as her hunger set in. She went to the bathroom counter, grabbed one of the plastic cups, poured herself a tall glass of sweet wine, and headed to the bed, ready to eat a few slices. Eve wondered how Vic managed to get the pizza and wine into her room and then thought to herself, that must have been why the clerk was so on edge. He was probably paid off and did not know why.

She laid there in bed, trying to sleep. Never had

her flashbacks seemed like an eternity. As she felt her consciousness ebbing away, the fear and the pain were as clear and concise as if they had happened mere moments ago. Her eyes were growing heavy from the strain. Finally, as her thoughts blurred, losing order and consistency, she gave in to her exhaustion. She was mentally dead to the world before the rest of her followed, slipping away into a restless sleep.

She woke a few times during the night. A few hours into her sleep, she woke coughing, covered in sweat, and believing she was back on the plank. The second time she was falling, inside a car with Campbell off a cliff. The image of the water before her was still playing over and over in her mind. She gave up sleeping and turned on the television. Eve was already not a fan of hotels. They never gave you enough coffee, the pillows were either too soft or too hard, and the blankets were as thin as the walls. She liked to have a window open or a fan, and hotels offered neither.

While Eve was struggling to sleep, the man she was looking for was also very much awake. He was in New York, just blocks from her hotel. He had just spent the day watching her. He saw her walking with the Muslim man with the robe and knew who he was, a terrorist. One of the four tried to blow up a Synagogue but was stopped by the FBI.

He guessed that Eve had gotten soft. She looked at the man, a religious man with a wife and children, and thought he deserved to live. Decisions should not be made based on emotion. He was not about to let this one go; he saw how she laughed and smiled at him. The two had been having such a good time.

When Eve gave up on any hope of sleep, she brewed herself a cup of coffee and ate a slice of pizza for breakfast. Although seeing an ex-lover was a slight detour from the mission, she felt compelled to do so. Before leaving for New York, Eve had contacted Judy, a friend from college, inviting her to lunch to catch up.

Judy was one of her college projects, a psychology experiment she had labeled Out of the Closet. Eve's plan was to help Judy recognize and accept her sexual preferences. She wanted to help Judy realize her full potential in that arena. It took nearly six months, and Eve was successful. Like her period in the company of Jim, once the mission was over, so was her time with Judy.

She arranged a meeting with Judy, not because she believed her ex-girlfriend was the killer, not at all. She did it more as a mission follow-up. Eve wanted to know how her influence, her involvement with Judy, had impacted her life. Speaking with Karl and Jim had made Eve feel pretty upbeat about the upcoming interaction. Both men had shown gratitude in a way she was not expecting. There was no doubt that Eve's manipulation of others was for good, not evil, but she was not so sure the ones she influenced understood that. Now she was beginning to think they did.

Eve was not ashamed of her time with Judy and saw herself as a lover. This did not mean she went around telling everyone she had dated a woman, but her secrecy was not out of shame. Once she started dating Franklin, she decided not to share information about her previous relationships with Franklin, or anyone.

Chapter Ten

Hey Jude

One of Eve's favorite things to do in New York that can't be done in Mobile was to go for ice cream after midnight in the winter. New York, a city that is equally exhausting, exhilarating, inspiring, and fast-paced, it is one of the most complex cities she could imagine living in. Still, the city becomes so much a part of you that one would never be content living anywhere else. One can blend into the environment, even while standing out, and for Eve, this was everything.

Today, wearing nothing more than a light jacket,

Eve took the subway to their meet-up spot. She had arranged to have lunch with Judy at the Community Food and Juice, a cafe emphasizing organic and vegetarian choices near Columbia, where Judy was now a professor teaching Art. Judy was raised in a religious household with parents who believed homosexuality should be one of the seven deadly sins, so 'coming out' in college was pretty difficult for her. Nevertheless, Eve was eager to find out if she would continue that path or revert back to her childhood religion and her parents' morals.

Eve selected a table outside. Although the weather was exceptional, the environment was a little overwhelming. Birds were swooping in, hoping for a stray crumb to feast on, leaving behind little packages no one wanted. Out- side the gate, the pavement was covered with squabbling, pecking pigeons and pedestrians maneuvering through the pigeon-people maze.

The noise from the traffic meant conversations were louder than usual, everyone using their outside voice. Eve could hear the neighbor's table talk. Inside, the café seemed calm by comparison. Eve soaked in the chaos. She missed New York and everything about it. The odors, the sounds, the whole environment. The heavy smell of exhaust fumes filled her nostrils, and the street just seemed to get busier with every moment, with people heading back to work, students carrying book bags, and couples walking hand-in-hand.

Seconds before Judy walked in, Eve received a text from Nadia. *Payton is dead.*

She sent a quick response asking how he died, hoping that this time the death was actually an accident.

When Judy walked in, she looked rather striking. She sported flawless skin, high cheekbones, white pixie hair, and a slender masculine body, very androgynous. She was dressed in a professorial, black, pinstriped suit, but with a lot of style.

The two embraced. After an exchange of greetings, they both ordered a beverage. Eve ordered a glass of wine and Judy a Manhattan.

"Judy, you look amazing." She said it and meant it. "You're looking pretty sexy yourself," said Judy, with confidence, Eve thought, so unlike the girl from college. "By the way, everyone calls me Jude," She sat back in her seat and had a far-off look in her eyes, "No one has called me Judy," she paused, thinking, "Since we dated." Then, after a short awkward moment, she added, "You seem distracted, on edge. Are you okay? Do I need to call someone?" Judy's ability to read people has improved as well.

Eve waved her hand dismissively, "No, I'm fine. Just a case I'm working on has me flustered. I work for the FBI now. Then she shifted gears, "How about you? Married?"

"My wife and I married several years ago, and we have a son and a daughter. It's been a bit of a challenge, he's got Down syndrome, and our little girl is autistic. We knew that when we adopted them."

"I have two kids myself and a husband. My daughter is two, and my son is...," Eve looked down at her watch,

"Two months old today. They're with my dad and his extended family."

The lunch was cordial, even after that awkward start. Eve was of the opinion that the conversation was a bizarre exchange of information rather than ex-lovers getting together. Eve knew she was keeping a distance and sounding a bit cold because she didn't want anything to happen to this woman. She was inclined to believe that if she exuded any kind of emotion toward Judy, she would end up dead.

Sure, that was an exaggeration. She didn't know and wasn't willing to take a chance. Eve told Jude about Jim, about him being in the hospital. Jude commented on Eve's unhappiness and asked if Jim's injury was why Eve had reached out to her.

About the time they were wrapping up and ready to go their separate ways, Eve received a text from Nadia. Hit and Run, it had to be our guy.

When she looked back up at Judy, Eve knew she had to tell her that her life may be in danger. This would not be an easy conversation.

"Judy, I mean Jude, I may have just put your life in danger."

Jude looked at Eve quizzically, "What do you mean you just put my life in danger? Is this still part of your undercover thing?" She paused. Eve did not reply. "Eve, am I really at risk? How is my life at risk?" Jude's nervousness was evident; she looked around and then back to Eve. "You better explain."

Eve told her about Campbell and Jim. She told Jude about visiting her old friend, Karl, who was still happy and healthy, and about Payton, killed in a hit and run just hours after their meeting.

"Why do you think my life is in danger? Were they all your ex-lovers?"

"No, just Jim, and well, you. I don't know if you're in danger. I have no idea why this person is hurting those you come into contact with, and I don't want anything to happen to you or your family. I will figure this out. In the meantime," Eve paused and then blurted, "You need to go away somewhere until this is over."

Jude stood up, "I can't believe you would risk my wife's and children's lives. You know, I tried to give you the benefit of the doubt, that maybe you cared about people, maybe you actually cared about me and just had a difficult time showing it," she pointed at Eve's chest, "That there was actually a heart in there! The fact is, you asked me to lunch knowing that this was a possibility. That just proves to me that you care only about yourself. I never want to see you again." She threw a fifty on the table, enough to cover her bill and Eve's, and walked out.

When the waiter came by, Eve ordered another glass of wine and a piece of chocolate cake. She had wanted cake for days, and she was finally going to have a piece. While she waited for the cake, she sent a text to Vic and asked if he'd be interested in getting a cup of coffee.

When the cake arrived, she had to take a minute or two before indulging, just to admire the chocolaty goodness. This lovely sweet thing was a twist on the childhood indulgence of chocolate bars when she went to town. This cake was no chocolate bar. Its Swiss vanilla frosting exterior was highlighted with dark sweet cherries and decorated with chocolate curls for visual appeal. The outside was tempting; the inside was just as glorious, a rich, moist, light, fluffy, sweet, melt-in-the-mouth, spongy goodness.

She ate her cake, enjoying every chocolaty bite, and noticed a man watching her. His stare was so obvious and intense that she could not help but stare back. It went on for so long that it became increasingly uncomfortable, and she thought he may be the one killing her friends and stalking her.

She was ready to stand up, walk over and confront him until something out of the corner of her eye made her turn around. Behind her, on the wall, was a big-screen television on mute, playing some sports event. Eve could only guess the teams. She didn't really keep up. What a close call. Eve stood up and gathered her things.

The route to the *Starbucks* Vic suggested was convoluted and lengthy, but Eve was up for it. She knew the NY subway system better than in her current neighborhood. The quickest way to get there was to take the subway, then it was a 38-minute ride. The total trip would take over two hours to walk and 45 minutes by taxi. It started with a short three-minute walk to the Cathedral Parkway 110 Street Station, two stops to the 96th street, and a minute walk to the *Brooklyn College* subway. Then, take it for eight stops to get to the Wall Street Station. Lastly, a mere two-minute walk to *Starbucks*, right around the corner from the *Museum of*

American Finance, now would be an excellent building to blow up. Eve wished she had brought her cane.

This *Starbucks* sold wine along with coffee. Want a glass of Pinot Noir, Carmel Road? Just twelve dollars. You can get a glass of Malbec with Chicken Skewers for only nine dollars. Definitely not your typical *Starbucks*, but then Wall Street is not your typical street.

Chapter Eleven

Visiting with Vic

Vic had been agreeable to a meeting and suggested the Wall Street *Starbucks*. That man was always surprising her. She was at that particular *Starbucks* when she triggered the bomb that took down the Wall Street insurance company headquarters and where she had watched the chaos unfold. Eve doubted their visit was a coincidence. How Vic knew this, she had no clue.

When she arrived, Vic was already there, and he had a coffee waiting for her. "You're looking a hell of a lot better since I last saw you." He handed her a Grande Sumatra,

"Your favorite."

"I don't think I could look much worse." Eve dwelt for just a second on her condition when pulled from the al-Fuqura compound. "If I'd been in there much longer, you wouldn't be looking at me. Your rescue was well-timed." She gave him a big smile, "And your dentist was amazing. I don't think my teeth ever looked this good"

"Forget about it. Now that I'm retired, I occasionally like a little excitement in my life. Let's just not make it a habit. I'm usually not in the rescue business. That seems to be Nadia's thing."

She took a drink of her coffee and let the lovely liquid slide down her throat. Eve felt the tension melt away. Mid-afternoon meant most New Yorkers were busy at work, so few people were around to annoy her. Eve admired the vintage photographs placed around the shop's wall, allowing customers to admire the photos and feel like they were living in a simpler time. Adding to the atmosphere were several dim lights, high above the nine-foot ceiling, creating a cozy environment yet still bright enough to shine on the furniture and strategically on the colorful products.

"All right, kiddo, lay it out. Let me know what's going on so we can brainstorm and see what we need to do next."

Eve told him about Payton, her unfortunate lunch with Judy, Jim in the hospital on life support, and Campbell dead.

"The ELF man?"

Eve laughed. He remembered her nickname for Campbell, "Yes, the ELF man is dead. Jim is nearly dead, and Payton is dead, all because of me. "Here's what the real issue is, Vic. I cannot for the life of me figure this out."

"Maybe you need more heads working on this. You know, I always thought you and Jackson looked good together. You were quite the couple, even if only for just one night. Why don't you bring him in? He lost his friend, so he's got a stake in the game. Give him a call."

"Are you kidding? Did you forget I framed them, and he knows it? There's no way he will want to work with me; besides, he's in prison."

"That's just an inconvenience and a minor one. You are FBI, after all, and it would surprise me if Nadia didn't have her own credentials. I'm sure you can get Jackson out legally or at least with the semblance of legality between the two of you."

"And Eve," he looked her in the eyes, "Jackson would make great bait to get the murderer out in the open."

"Hmm... that's not a bad idea. What are the chances that he would go along with it?"

"Let's just assume he says yes, and you get him to help you. Who else is on the list that you need to visit?"

"The Aryan Nation guys, you know, the ones that helped me with the Hutaree problem."

"Eve, Doll, remind me, what was the Hutaree problem? I'm getting old, and my memory is not what it used to be."

"Joshua Carter, the leader of the Michigan militia group. I interviewed him at the conference and found him a sick, abusive pedophile, so I casually suggested to the Aryan Nation guys that they protect my honor or some shit like that. They did. They beat and ultimately killed him.

His body was taken back to Michigan, and I made it up there in time to attend his funeral and arrange to meet his wife and kids and take them away. Nadia and I went together the morning after the funeral and did just that. Thanks to Nadia, we freed all the women and children interested in leaving that awful place and brought them back to Tres Piedras. Eve thought about that day often, especially when questioned the value of life she placed on others. Eve knew she was oversharing, and while she really liked Vic, she didn't know much about him.

"Oh yes, now I remember The Hutaree guy, Mr. Carter. I really think you should contact Jackson."

"Fine. As soon as I get back to my dad's place, Nadia and I will work something out." Their coffee was finished, and Eve had another plane to catch. Vic offered a ride to the airport.

While waiting at the airport, she had plenty of time to evaluate her life and career choices. Eve thought back to her time as Dr. Nicole Mathers. What she liked best about going undercover was the ability to start over fresh and create a past with only good moments and happy memories, even if imaginary. When she was Dr. Nicole, she was not a little girl whose mother abandoned her. She was never a high school student who felt so utterly alone that, at times, she wondered if life was worth it. She was not a woman that hid behind black clothes and a badge. As Nicole Mathers, she was an accomplished professional with a pleasant upbringing.

Eve's first undercover job was working at a bank as a

teller. That job was literally the most boring job ever. She didn't know how bank employees handled the monotony. It took her three days to figure out that the unsub was one of the loan officers. He was angry because he had been passed over for promotion in favor of less experienced employees who had degrees while he did not. The man had given the bank ten years of his life. The guy thought time on the job was enough. He started dating an easily manipulated bank teller and convinced her that if she stole enough money, he would marry her, and they would run off together. He lied. So, she, the spurned lover, confessed.

Eve's second undercover job put her on the streets of Los Angeles. Girls were being lifted off the street and trafficked across state lines. Fortunately for the Johns, she was not tasked to work the streets, just observe and report. The guys were taking girls as young as twelve. Eve had noticed a pattern; they were picking them up on different streets, depending on the day of the week. Five different men were picking up the girls. Each man had a particular taste in looks and age. It had been simple for Eve to identify the patterns and predict who would be the next victim. She was there to bust the creep when it happened. He was easy to flip, and before the week ended, the ring was busted.

There had been a few others, and in all cases, she got her man or woman. Eve was utterly flummoxed by how she could not figure out who was stalking her and killing everyone in her wake. It's likely she was too close to the subjects and worked better when she was outside looking in. Maybe she needed to think more like an outsider to find the pattern. Campbell and Payton were killed, and Jim and I were injured. Karl and Jude were untouched.

Campbell and Payton were terrorists. Jim, Karl, Jude, and I was not. Except he tried to kill Jim twice. Campbell, Jim, and Payton and my trip to al-Fuqura were planned trips, with phone calls and emails exchanged.

Jude was tagged on to the trip for Payton, and Karl was just a drive. If Eve were to make an educated guess, she would say someone had hacked her email and cell phone accounts. If she wanted to create a trap, she would plan a trip, fly there, meet with a male, and spend time with him. Then, the male followed until the killer was caught. Simple. Now she just had to find someone to use as bait. Jackson. Vic's suggestion sounded like a good idea.

Chapter Twelve

Jackson Jail Break

Eve phoned her father and shared her plan to break Jackson out of jail and use him for bait. By the time she made it back to Tres Piedras, he had done all the preliminary research and collected the information they needed to get started.

"*The Lebanon Correctional Institute* is operated by the Ohio Department of Rehabilitation and Corrections in Warren County, Ohio. Just to give you some reference points, that's about four miles west of Lebanon and two miles east of Monroe, which is about thirty-two miles north of Cincinnati. You can fly in at the Cincinnati Airport and get a rental car. The prison sits on 1900 acres. Much of that is used as a farm, and inmates work the farm and learn skills like food production." He looked up at his daughter, "Those are good skills. This has probably been good for him to be there."

Eve did not seem amused, but John knew she appreciated the effort. He carried on. "It has 2500 inmates, 580 staff, 340 of those are security. Did I mention it's a minimum-security prison, so he likely has free reign of the place? This won't negate the fact that he's going to be really upset with you."

"Now, as far as why he went to jail and Payton didn't. What I found was the Payton had no priors, except the entrapment debacle, whereas when Jackson's room was searched, they found a weapon that he had purchased in Cincinnati and taken across state lines to New York. In addition to that, he had a felony for an attempted robbery at the age of eighteen, which precludes him from being able to own a weapon. Not only did he get arrested for having a weapon in his possession when he arrived at the New York City hotel; he had time added because he bought the weapon in Ohio."

"Now the good news is that he only got eight years, three of which he has served despite both charges and convictions. He's eligible for parole next year." John paused, making sure she was absorbing it all, "What I think we should do, and correct me if you have other ideas, is to put together a document from the FBI stating that early release is necessary because he is pivotal in a case for the FBI. If you can come up with a draft letter using FBI verbiage, I will make it look authentic. Then you and Nadia will head out there and see how he feels about becoming bait."

"Dad, why should Nadia come with me? I can handle this alone, and she may be needed here in case the killer shows up in Tres Piedras to do something to you guys."

"Not this again, Eve," said John, sounding annoyed. "I have the village taking care of us, and we have the bunker if anything happens. We're safe; however, you've been too close to each of these events, and I don't want to risk you leaving Tres Piedras again without your own backup. So that means she's going with you."

Eve knew better than to argue with her father, especially as Nadia had just walked into the living room with a gym bag, saying she was ready to go.

"You're a little premature, Nadia. We still have a lot of details to work out. Besides, I need to spend some time with my kids. Let me figure out this document for dad," She reached into her bag and pulled out her laptop, "And spend the evening with them. We can head out tomorrow. Dad, can you arrange the flights again?" Man, she really hated flying. It had felt like she had lived in the air during the past few weeks.

The next morning Eve and Nadia landed at the Cincinnati National Airport and rented a Chevrolet Suburban, the most common vehicle used by the Bureau, to get them to the Lebanon Correctional Facility. Eve was in full FBI mode. Her suit, shoes, even her hair, and sunglasses all shouted FBI. At the facility, she walked up to the gate, flashed her badge, and said she needed to speak to the warden.

Once inside, she informed the prison staff that she was there to collect a prisoner. The two women were ushered into a room, and the staffers rushed away to figure out how to proceed. The room smelled of varnish and wood, with a hint of tobacco. There were two windows too high to see out of unless standing on tiptoe. The windows admitted a nebulous, gauzy light, cut through by two sets of florescent lights flickering and emitting a strange buzzing noise.

One wall was covered mainly by a large scratched whiteboard. Years of use had left indelible marks, destined to remain, heedless of attempts to erase. The tray held several markers. In front of the whiteboard was a skinny rectangular metal table with rusted legs and a laminate marble surface freckled with coffee stains. On top of the table was a box full of colorful Post-it notes, stacks of them.

Eve and Nadia sat in two of the plastic seats organized like a schoolroom, rows of chairs with an aisle separating the sides. The floor was a wooden plank, waxed to a high shine. A dingy American flag hung limply in the corner left of the whiteboard. A metal trash can with flaking gray paint sat in the corner. Nadia, feeling rather bored, started wadding up the paper squares and attempting to make baskets. The Post-it notes were too light and littered the floor inches away.

Eve took the Post-its and created origami animal art. Her ducks and swans looked like no animals ever seen before. They both laughed at the misshapen creatures, and Eve had to identify each species for Nadia. Nadia started throwing the paper animals in the direction of the trash basket and ranked them by the ones that made it closest, "Eve, your swan is in the lead. Quick, make a turtle."

It felt like hours before a bad-tempered, overweight male officer, smelling of pizza and pipe tobacco, came to escort them to see the warden. He saw the Post-it notes crumpled and tossed throughout the room. He gave them a quizzical look but chose not to question the FBI agent or the woman accompanying her. Finally, they made their way to the warden's office.

In the time it took to get there, the warden was briefed on their visit, and when the two women walked in, she introduced herself and shook their hands. Then she held her hand out for the document stating that the release of Jackson was sanctioned by Eve's superiors. Fortunately for Eve, this document is not one many wardens would have seen before.

As indicated in the document, the high-security nature of the prisoner's release made it unlikely she would try to contact Eve's superiors. There was no reason for the warden to question the letter's authenticity. Besides, the letter was allegedly signed by the FBI director, so she would have to go pretty high up the food chain to verify the document. Eve doubted she would even know where to begin. Local law avoided interaction with the FBI as much as possible.

Eve stared at the warden, a woman who ruled over a prison. She was as beautiful as anyone in Hollywood. Her thick, wavy, black hair fell gracefully down her shoulders and encircled her round face. Her golden-brown skin tone showed off her smooth, clear complexion, high cheekbones, and brilliant white teeth. The warden's slightly arched, chestnut-colored eyebrows moved up and down as she scanned the letter. Intelligent, large, dark eyes spoke volumes about the will of the woman, that she was a strong-minded and resolute individual that presented with strength and confidence that Eve was sure the prison staff recognized.

The warden made a phone call and instructed the person on the other end to get prisoner 2204 prepared for release. When she hung up the phone, she asked the ladies if they would like something to drink. Then, she rang a bell, and in walked her assistant, a smiling, older woman with a tray holding a coffee pot, cups, and cookies. This warden certainly knows how to make her guests feel at home. It's probably because she's a woman, Eve mused. Women go that extra step.

There was a lot of small talk about the weather and national politics. Then the warden excused herself for a few minutes. Eve and Nadia thought there was a chance that their ruse was up, they were busted, and the coffee was just a ploy to keep them here. However, their fears were abated when she returned, smiling, and said that Jackson was ready and could they please follow her.

Eve's focus was shattered. She was filled with nervous anticipation and wasn't convinced she could form complete sentences. Her thoughts branched out in infinite directions. She had to get through the day in one piece. Eve was going to see the man that she had unintentionally put behind bars, the one that had given her the best sex of her life. She was pretty sure it wasn't going to turn out as lovely of a reunion as she would like, but as long as her emotions took a backseat in the conversation, she should be able to make him understand. She took a deep breath.

There he was, walking down the hall. She hadn't seen him in years, and she was struck anew by his good looks. He had been an attractive man, tall, with a groomed mane of black hair. His hair was now frosted with gray but thick, with an unruliness that came from the inexperienced barbers, found inside a prison. She noticed that his figure had been hardened by his time behind bars, and he carried his height with the same easy self- assurance she remembered. His steel-blue eyes looked both cold and calculating. It added to his attractiveness, hinting at the untamed individual underneath. He had a swagger she didn't recall seeing before and a toughness about him that she did remember. That sexy body, and his voice, his deep voice. She was putting herself in a mood where she had no business going, so she quickly shrugged it off.

When he got close, the guards that escorted him to the exit fell back, and the warden shook Jackson's hand. "Son, it looks like this is your lucky day, this lovely FBI agent and her Israeli counterpart are here to take you into their custody. Hopefully, with them, you can turn your life around, make some changes for the good and serve your country."

Jackson looked mystified. What the hell? Dr. Mathers and FBI? This was getting more confusing by the minute, but he let it go, at least for now. He shook the warden's hand and thanked her.

The three walked to the black SUV with both the ladies flanking him. No words were spoken until they were in the car. Eve's smile continued to grow despite her attempts to remain neutral. She wanted to be in control of either letting him see what he ignited in her or choosing to hide it. Either way, he was the most fun thing she had in her world at the moment.

Nadia was in the back seat with Eve's firearm pointed directly at Jackson in the seat in front of her. She was disappointed with Eve's choice of weapon, the Glock, a blocky, black pistol designed for simplicity and dependable to a fault. The Glock comes in several models, but they all look and feel the same. The only thing she liked about the weapon was the grip enhancer.

As soon as they were away from the prison, Jackson let her have it. "Nicole, what's going on? How did you get me out of jail? Why are they calling you an FBI agent?"

"First off, my name's not Nicole. It's Eve, Special Agent Evelyn Black."

There was about a five minutes silence before he spoke again, "Were you working undercover at the conference?"

"Yes."

"And you and me, that night, that was part of your undercover work?" He asked in an almost disgusted tone.

"No, it wasn't, in fact, that dalliance cost me a promotion and had me transferred to Alabama from New York." He need not know the real details.

"What about the hotel, my sunglasses, the bombs, the gun? Was that the FBI trying to frame us again, using you to make it happen?"

"Frame you again? Jackson, I saw the video and heard the tapes. You may be able to convince a jury you were entrapped, but let's not lie here."

Eve was not about to tell Jackson everything, but she

did tell him that she didn't mean for him to go to jail. At the time, she had been unaware of the felony on his record or that he had a weapon and had no reason to think he would be charged or convicted of a crime.

"But let me see if I have this straight, you're saying you meant to get Jim and Bill in prison?"

"It's really difficult, and I can't give you all the details. It's classified. I can just say you were not supposed to go to prison."

Another bout of silence. Eve knew Jackson was processing what she had told him. Before they reached the airport, Eve felt compelled to tell him about Payton.

"Jackson, this is hard for me to tell you. I planned on getting you released once I worked out how to make it happen. Things have been sped up because someone killed Payton yesterday. The accident this time was reported as a hit-and-run. I believe the same person is targeting everyone I interviewed. I was even set up to be tortured and killed. Luckily the woman in the back seat rescued me before they finished me off. I want to find out who's doing this before more people die."

"You have to be kidding me. You betrayed my friends and me for the last three years, and you, Special Agent Eve Black, left me to rot in jail." Jackson growled at her. "Is this even an actual release or some sick game you're playing with me? My best friend is dead because of you, and my life is in danger, all thanks to you. Now you're asking me to help you?" He paused, and his eyes narrowed, "And if I say no, you put me back in prison. That's how this works, right?"

He's certainly not over it; this will take some time. Eve gave an audible sigh, "Jackson, the choice is yours, one hundred percent up to you. If you want to go your own way right now, I'll stop the car, and you can go. I'll give you the paperwork, money, anything you need... but I hope you decide to work with us."

"Stop the car."

"Seriously?" Eve braked and signaled to the shoulder. "Yes, stop the goddamn car right now."

Eve pulled to the side of the road and came to a stop. Jackson clutched the handle on the door to open it, but nothing happened. He turned around and glared at Eve, "Am I your prisoner?"

"No, it automatically locks," she clicked the unlock lever on her door, "Try it now." It worked for him this time.

Before stepping out of the car, he reached out to her. She was relieved and went to take his hand, but he pulled his back. "I want all those things you just said you'd give me."

Jackson was nervous. He knew the lady in the back seat had a gun pointed at him. He did not need to see it to know it was there. At any minute, he expected to feel the metal of a weapon in contact with the back of his head, but he wasn't about to help these people that put him behind bars. Eve reached into her bag, pulled out a large ivory business envelope and her wallet, grabbed all the cash she had, and handed them both to him.

He looked at her hands, her clean nails, free of polish, and wearing a suit that looked nothing like the clothes she wore when they last met. When he took the envelope, he met her eyes, and their hands touched briefly. Time stopped. Suddenly he didn't want to go.

He took both the envelope and the money, then hurriedly exited the car, slamming the door. Jackson started to walk in the opposite direction with no idea where he was or where he was going.

Before he could take more than a couple steps, the woman in the back seat rolled down her window and tossed him a phone. "Call the only number in the contacts if you need anything."

He shoved it in his pocket and walked away. With each step, he started to believe that he might actually be free. Jackson noticed everything, the wind on his face, the sound of birds and traffic... he was out. What he didn't know was where to go. His mother had died some years ago, and his best friend had just been killed. No one cared that he was out of jail, except maybe the woman that just drove away.

The upcoming town was not far, and it looked like Nicole had given him close to three hundred dollars. He would find a place to spend the night and see what came up tomorrow. Jackson was pumped, the day was warm, and he had not been free to do this for a few years. About three miles into the walk, he was getting tired. At five miles, his fatigue turned to anger, but before he made it to mile six, he came across a motel with rooms for less than fifty a night.

Across from the motel were an all-night Steak 'n Shake and a gas station. He ordered himself a hamburger and fries and then bought a six-pack and carried it back to his room. Jackson had decided before getting out of the car that his time with Nicole/Eve was not over, but that reunion had to be done on his terms.

The hotel was nothing special. The lobby had the same smell as an old person's home. The carpet was out of date, with worn patches defining the path to the desk. On the wall was a print of a large fruit bowl, as old and yellowed as the carpet. The floor-to-ceiling windows should allow a lot of light through, yet the heavy drapes and city dirt on the panes left it dull to the point of depression. Jackson didn't have high expectations; he just wanted a place to lay his head and to celebrate his first night out of jail. At least it wasn't one of those seedy pay-by-the-hour places full of whores and desperate men.

The room itself was old but clean. He noted the same carpet that he saw in the lobby, without the worn spots. The bed was soft, the sheets fresh, and the television worked. He threw his bag on the table and slumped into the nearby armchair. There was something so great about being in a space that allowed him to do as he pleased. He reached down and pulled off his shoes, socks, and jeans. Wearing only a shirt and boxers, he felt even freer. Popping off the lid and taking a long pull on the bottle of beer reminded him of old times that were not necessarily good times. His eyes settled on the envelope, and the phone Nicole's friend had given him. He kept forgetting that she was not Nicole. She was Eve, the beautiful, badge-wearing, gun-toting Eve.

After a few beers, his eyes were heavy, and he wanted a warm shower by himself. He pulled off his remaining clothes as he headed to the bathroom. His body responded to the warm water, and his thoughts kept returning to

Eve, to Payton, and then back to Eve. Jackson let out a scream as, all at once, the water went from pleasantly warm to freezing his balls off. He had no choice but to get out and dry off before slipping into the warm bed. Sleep came easy but didn't last long.

It took him less than twenty-four hours to decide he was bored, and he texted Eve, "I'm in." She responded, telling him to get back to the airport and a ticket would be waiting for him. He did not even ask where he was going. He just knew he was ready to kick some ass.

Jackson's initial anger and distrust had not come as a surprise to Eve. She knew the man intimately. Jackson was not innocent; he had a violent past and would likely not hesitate to kill anyone that got in his way. He was deep and serious on the surface, but when Eve and he were alone, there was a playful, fun side.

Eve admitted that she had done her research and knew he could be a scary person, but she saw his human side too. She figured as a kid, he grew up learning that he had to be strong, to take care of his people at all costs. He could come across as cold, extremely cocky, and very confident. A man like that doesn't make decisions without thinking about all the options. Inside the envelope, she had given him was her contact information. Eve knew he would call; it would just be on his own terms, at his own time.

Chapter Thirteen

Girl Talk

They were heading north to Ulysses, Pennsylvania. The village had been taken over by the Aryan Nation. There she would find the four thugs she had interviewed in Cincinnati, the ones she so easily convinced to kill the Hutaree leader, Joshua Carter. The drive would take seven hours. Eve would take the first shift, and Nadia would take the second.

The two passed through Columbus and Cleveland, switching drivers at that point to sleep. The traffic was light on I71 along Lake Erie, passing through the

Allegheny National Forest to the *Laurelwood Inn and Steakhouse,* southwest of Ulysses.

The *Laurelwood Inn* was located in Coudersport, PA, north of places like *Sweden Valley and Coudersport Ice Mine,* which conjured images of places much further north. The GPS had trouble finding the Inn, but Nadia and Eve were okay with that. If the GPS had difficulty, anyone potentially following them would have trouble as well.

There was only one other car in the parking lot. The other guests apparently all drove motorcycles. At a glance, she counted at least twenty different sizes, styles, and models. Eve had no idea how to drive a motorcycle, but she had a feeling Nadia would be experienced. That woman could do anything.

When Eve walked into the lobby, she looked around, at first a little worried that she had just walked into someone's living room. There was a worn beige sofa, thread bare in some areas, with dark green throw pillows. A light oak coffee table was placed in front of it, the top littered with advertisements.

A pleather lounger was next to the sofa, in the nut-brown with a plaid throw draped over the back. In case someone felt like napping, she thought. What an interesting idea. The room was very clean, and there was a smiling young person behind the counter.

She paid for a room with two double beds, and the place was unbelievably affordable. Eve had no idea you could stay at places so cheaply. It must be a Midwestern thing. When they made it to their room, Nadia threw her bag on the bed closest to the door and headed straight to the bathroom, "I need a shower."

When she finally emerged from the bathroom several minutes later, she had one towel draped around her and one clutched in her hand, and Eve just watched as she aggressively dried her hair. "The water pressure was intense, almost massage-like. The bathroom itself is very small, you may get a little claustrophobic, also no outlets, and you'll have to request more towels, sorry."

Eve was too tired to return to the lobby to request more towels, so she looked about and found a spare blanket, "No problem, I'll use this," showing Nadia the neatly folded, baby blue acrylic blanket. "It's a blanket. It has to be absorbent." It didn't do as good a job as she would've liked, but she was showered, and her hair was nearly clean; Nadia had used the toiletry shampoo, the whole bottle, so Eve was forced to use the facial soap on her hair as well as her face. She knew her hair was going to frizz with no conditioner, so she poured a little of the complementary hand lotion onto her palm and ran it through her auburn hair.

As she lay in bed, fully prepared to sleep for a few hours, she noticed the sun was just starting to rise, naturally lightening the room. The beige blinds on the windows were old and missing slats. Eve was convinced she could sunbathe right on her bed. She put the spare pillow over her eyes, hoping it would do the trick, and that was when she realized the walls were very thin. She could hear people waking in other rooms and a strange noise coming from an old factory down the road.

Eve had heard it when they first arrived, but she was distracted by everything else. Now, as she lay in the bed, the noise was all she could think about. She wrapped the pillow around her face to cover her ears. The thin pillow proved inadequate at blocking the noise.

Good thoughts, she told herself. The mattresses were new and firm. The white sheets were soft and gave the appearance of being immaculately clean and sanitary. The room needed a remodel. The TV was a huge bulky thing sitting on a desk. The room was clean, cheap, and comfortable. Eve knew she was going to miss the free continental breakfast, so she had grabbed a couple donuts from the lobby after getting her key, and now their frosty sweet glazed goodness was calling out to her. She was now hungry and bored.

"Nadia, are you awake?"

Next, Eve heard a muffled and groggy, "Yes."

"Have you always liked older men?"

Nadia's eyes opened, and she knew she was not going to be sleeping any time soon. Eve had slept while she drove the last three hours and was probably feeling wide awake, whereas Nadia just wanted to sleep.

"Yes, Eve, I have ever only dated older men."

"How old were you when you had your first boyfriend?"

Nadia sat up, looked over at Eve, and found her sitting cross-legged on her bed, eating a donut and smiling at her with a smudge of jelly on her cheek.

Nadia got up out of bed and walked into the bathroom, returning with a damp washcloth and throwing it at Eve.

"For your face, now give me the other donut. I was seventeen, I dated one of my trainers, he was twenty-six, and before you ask, no, we were not breaking laws. The Israeli military service has no specific regulations forbidding fraternization. What about you?"

"My first real boyfriend was Jim."

Nadia thought she detected some emotion, maybe sadness, in that sentence. She thought about what Eve must be feeling. Jim was now in so much pain and scarred for life, and Eve was the cause. "It must be really hard for you, with Jim in the hospital, and he was your first."

"I don't understand," Eve licked jelly off of her thumb and cocked her head at Nadia, "Why hard for me? He's the one in the hospital, not me."

"I know, Eve, I'm just saying that I understand how you must be feeling, guilt, sadness...." She trailed off.

Eve shrugged and replied unconvincingly, "Sure, I feel sad."

Nadia paused before saying. "Actually, Eve, I don't think you do."

"Do what?" "Feel sad."

There was a long silence before they spoke again.

"I don't know, Nadia. It's possible I don't feel like everyone else; I have been faking it for so long now it's hard to know what is real and what stems from years of practice."

"Do you think you are a sociopath?"

"Wow, I can't believe you just asked me that." She was unsure how to continue, "Do you think I am?"

"I really don't know. I have been trying to figure it out practically from the first day we met. I think you care for people. I have witnessed you get upset when people are abused, like Mari's family, and I have watched you help people without gaining anything in return; however, sometimes, just sometimes, your emotions don't line up with what I would expect. You consistently look content when others are in pain, and you don't seem truly upset when people experience trauma. Like Jim, for example, he is in the hospital because of you, and he was your first boyfriend, yet your immediate response was not to cry or to feel empathy for what he is going through. All you've done is seek revenge. Like he was your property, and someone broke it."

She paused, giving Eve a chance to say something. When Eve didn't, she continued. "In fact, it appears to me that the only time you show real emotion is when something belonging to you is being hurt, neglected, abused, or taken away. Then you do something selfless, and I think I must be wrong. I just can't read you."

"I don't know how to answer you, Nadia, but if it helps, I wonder myself."

"Do you feel anything about Campbell's death? I know you didn't know him as well as you knew Jim, but you spent time together, you laughed and talked about passionate things, and you said he reminded you of John. Do you miss him? Do you feel like crying but are holding back? Do you think about what it must have felt like for him knowing he was dying? Any of those things cross your mind?"

Eve debated on how to respond. If she told her the answer to all those things, would Nadia be repelled by her? Would she no longer trust her? "I think I just compartmentalize better than most people, Nadia. Now let's try to sleep. I'm tired."

Nadia knew Eve was trying to avoid taking the discussion any further, but she let it go.

When they at last woke, the two acted like the exchange had never happened. Eve grumbled about the bad coffee. Nadia objected to her complaining.

Eve applied enough makeup to hide the bruising on her face. The last thing she wanted to do was to explain to the Aryan Nation guys what happened. She knew that would just rile them and distract them from the mission. Before they left, Eve ran down to the lobby to secure the room for another night and to check to see if there were any more donuts. There were none.

When she returned, Nadia was packed and waiting. Eve emptied out her FBI credentials, license, and any other potential identifiers and put them into one of the room's pillowcases. She then took the pen off the desk, broke off the clip, and walked into the bathroom.

Eve stood on the toilet, and with Nadia holding her steady, she unscrewed the vent and put the pillowcase inside. With just a hand-tightening of the screws, they were done. After one more quick look around the room, Eve felt satisfied that her identity was safe, and they left.

Nadia took the driver's seat. She knew if she was going to be around Eve all day, the first thing she had to do was get her some good coffee and something decent to eat. The closest *Starbucks* was over an hour away. Nadia had checked before they left. There was a café nearby, the *Olga Gallery, Cafe, & Bistro*. It sounded like a place that could not decide what it wanted to be, like the *Laurelwood Inn and Steakhouse*. The reviewers complimented the coffee, the food, and the décor. Eve would just have to be satisfied with that.

Their timing was once again spot on. The lunch crowd was gone, leaving them the ability to sit away from people so they could speak without eavesdroppers. The gallery section did not include portraits and landscapes hanging on walls. The work was, as they put it, 'Seriously good art,' including jewelry, hand-knits, and quilts. Nadia tried not to laugh. On the front of the menu, she read about the history of the place. *Olga's Gift Boutique* started with just exquisite *Ukrainian Eggs by Olga*.

The talented lady tried her hand at the hand-painted glass, acrylic painting, knitted yarn creations, hand-made jewelry, and various multi-media kits. Her husband John was responsible for the café. Nadia finally understood that at both locations, the owners were husband and wife teams working together to build a space they could both be passionate about. She no longer wanted to laugh. She envied Olga and John,

Christine, and Paul, and their relationships.

As soon as they had awakened, Eve had started checking her phone, hoping for a text from Jackson. There was nothing. At one point during lunch, Nadia grabbed the phone out of her hands and said, "No phones at the table." Which worked for a short time, but once their plates were empty, she was back at it. Nadia did her best to ignore it and mentally worked on the plan as she drove the twenty minutes to Ulysses.

Chapter Fourteen

Aryan Nation

August Kreis III was the name of the man that had first made Ulysses the national headquarters of the Aryan Nations group, but he was just one of several prominent white supremacist groups that called Ulysses home. They would not be meeting Mr. Kreis because he was serving fifty years on a child-molestation conviction.

As they approached Ulysses, Pennsylvania, from the south, the first thing Nadia saw was the town's welcome sign with a population of 650. Above that was a traffic sign with a silhouette of a horse-drawn cart, reminding drivers that the Amish use the roads too. Nadia knew about people like the Amish that turned their back on modern amenities but had yet to meet one.

Nadia looked around. She had expected people walking on the streets, shopping with toddlers in tow, banners and bright store signs, and lively small-town businesses, but she saw nothing of the sort. What she saw was an empty old town with a country market and Ace Hardware, an old bank shop, a community center, and a church. All with a feel of a town desperately in need of repair and was eerily quiet, like the start of a scary movie. Time appeared to slow down here. As they passed downtown, they saw people sitting on their front porches lazily waving at cars going by.

Ulysses was not like other small towns; this town received national attention because of the hate groups that called it home. She tried to relate it to her only U.S. small-town experience, Tres Piedras. Nadia knew that strong emotions lead to ample opportunity for genuine conflict on a very personal level.

Hate could become an ingrained way of life between the people of the town and the extremist groups that congregated in the geographic area surrounding Ulysses, and even between the individual hate groups themselves. Long-standing feuds seem to be the norm in U.S. rural areas, but she was also aware of the fierce protectiveness among townspeople and hate groups, the 'we take care of our own' mentality that can lead to narrow-mindedness and conflict.

In a city, there is anonymity, but in a small town like this one, everyone knows everyone. There was comfort in knowing everyone, but this could be seen as a double-edged sword. Neighbors became almost like extended family. Personal business and the networks of relationships became a little too intimate, and gossip was rampant. There was rarely an opportunity to meet anyone new. The youngest members in small towns are often quite anxious to get out, to go off to college, join the military, to do whatever it takes to escape their all too familiar life, only to ache for it during troubled times.

As Eve and Nadia made their way to the north side of town, along the main thoroughfare, they saw a home dedicated to the memory of Adolf Hitler. Nazi flags on tall poles and wooden swastikas stood in the yard amongst other debris. It looked messy, poor, and unclean. Nadia wondered aloud if they had bathrooms or were still using outhouses.

Eve laughed, but she remembered when she and her father lived like that, with no showers and very few opportunities to be clean. That was when they had first moved to New Mexico and looked like a band of intellectuals living a gypsy lifestyle. This lifestyle was common; many people were doing it in the early 1970s. She often thought of the people from the nearby towns, but never did she contemplate what they thought of her or the Socialist for Humanity party.

Eve began to read aloud the Aryan Nation fact sheet her father had prepared for them. "White supremacy got its foothold in Ulysses and Potter County over a hundred years ago with the arrival of the Ku Klux Klan, giving the town national significance." She had read that in the mid-2000s, it hosted the World Aryan Congress, a gathering of neo-Nazis, skinheads and Klan members.

He had included an FBI report. How does he find these things? "Six members of the Aryan Strike Force cell were arrested and charged with weapons and drug offenses. One member, a terminally ill man, planned a suicide attack at an anti-racist protest. He was prepared to hide a bomb in his oxygen tank and blow himself up, along with other protesters." The group had conducted weapons training at the Farm in Ulysses, the place they were heading to now.

If Nadia had her way, she would just bomb the whole town. She had never understood the hate that groups like these felt against her people. She had heard it all. Jews were targeted because they were too liberal and also because they were too conservative. They were too cheap and had too much money, causing envy in others. They were too passive or pushy, too charitable and too selfish, and too religious or not religious enough. The inconsistencies were crushing. The Jewish people were the scapegoats for all things people hated. Heading into a town full of racist idiots with guns made her very nervous.

They timed their arrival at the farm to be late afternoon or early evening. They knew this was the right place, graffiti announcing the philosophy of hate visible on all the buildings: White Nation, White Pride, Skin Heads, 88, 814, and other symbols that meant nothing to her.

They slowed as they approached two men blocking the road. As soon as Eve said her name, Dr. Nicole Mathers, she saw a glimpse of recognition in the guy's eye. He told the other guard to find Bobby or Matt. The other two were off running errands.

She didn't know them by name, but as soon as they

approached, Eve recognized them, and she assumed by their big smiles that they recognized her as well.

"Well, hey doctor, good to see you again. What brings you here?"

"You guys did say if I was ever in the neighborhood that I should stop by." She flashed them a coy smile. While neither of them recalled saying something like that, they believed her.

"Who's your friend?" The other one asked, giving Nadia the once over.

"This is Nadia, my father's girlfriend. I was in an accident recently," Eve held up her cane, "Nadia has been helping me get around."

"Don't you talk?" One of the Aryan Nation men asked Nadia. Of course, she talked, but more than talking, what she wanted to do was blow the brains out of these anti-Semitic assholes.

She couldn't really say that, so she just nodded her head and, in her best American accent, said, "It is very nice to meet the both of you."

Eve noted the accent change and thought, of course, she's Jewish, and we just entered a camp that hates Jewish people. Eve had not even considered the risk she was putting Nadia in, rookie mistake. But Nadia had, and in time to avert a potential disaster.

"Come have some dinner with us," the one called Bobby said. "We have a really good cook. He used to work at a truck stop out on PA49. His chicken and hamburgers are the best, but I think he's off tonight, so the fixings may not be as good, but we have plenty."

They both agreed to join Bobby and the others, so they could have an excuse to walk around the farm and get an assessment of the people living there. It appeared to Eve that her cover was not blown, so she could cross these guys off her list.

Before they walked another step, the gate guard told Bobby and Matt that the guests would need to be patted down before they could go on their white land. Eve and Nadia were expecting a search, so they left their weapons in their locked rental car and her FBI credentials in the motel.

The guard made Eve uncomfortable. He had an oily voice, greased back hair, and piercing dark eyes that looked at her like a wolf might observe its prey. The inspection started at Eve's neck, squeezing a little too tight before he worked his way down the arms to her fingers and then back up to her armpits.

She stood there rigid, resisting the urge to punch him as he then, after taking a deep breath, ran his arms over her breasts, and in her opinion, too long there, as well as on her ass. He told her to spread her legs, making it sound as lewd as he could. Once spread, he felt up both the inside and the outside, down to her feet. Eve wanted a shower.

When he was done with Eve, he moved on to Nadia. She did not appear to be put out as much as Eve. In fact, Eve gave her a WTF look. She seemed to be enjoying it! Her body seemed to quiver under his hands, and once, she made a slight noise of pleasure. When he was done the whole act appeared very seductive and inviting. Eve knew Nadia was just throwing them off her "Jewish" scent, but she also knew regardless of the reason, she could never fake it as well as she had just witnessed Nadia doing.

The man appeared delighted that he was able to receive such encouragement and thought later, if they decided to stay the night, he would visit her bed, whether she wanted it or not. He gave a knowing nod to Bobby. The group, Bobby, Matt, Eve, and Nadia, walked toward a prefabricated, metal building near the farmhouse.

It appeared to be some sort of headquarters, game room, and lunch hall for the members. There was an echo in the space. The dinner was buffet-style, but the selection was small. The choices were canned soup, PB&J sandwiches, chips, rolls, and canned soda or beer. Bottled water was not an option. Nadia played around with her food without eating a thing. Eve ate it all.

Nadia knew she was behind enemy lines, so she was preparing herself for anything out of the normal. Not Eve. She was relaxed. They were still calling her Dr. Nicole or sister, and besides, she really liked the food.

The conversation was polite. Eve shared with the men how they had visited the Hutaree compound and rescued some girls. They looked at Nadia with a new amount of appreciation. After dinner, the men offered up a couple rooms for the girls and were not going to take no for an answer. The two agreed to stay at the compound for the night, ignoring their inner voices, and told the men they would have to leave very early in the morning.

Neither Eve nor Nadia liked the idea of sleeping in separate rooms, but neither wanted to show their hosts how uncomfortable they were. They didn't feel the need to offend the Neanderthals.

Around 1 A.M., Nadia woke, she knew someone was in her room, and while she hoped Eve was making this middle of the night visit, she knew better. Eve would have identified herself right away. This surprise visit was not unexpected, and being prepared meant she was fully dressed under the blankets.

Nadia listened without breathing to the sound of someone removing shoes and unzipping their pants. She was pretty sure the intruder was the groping guard and was pleased she had pinched a knife at dinner and had it under her pillow ready to use. The room was pitch black, so when Nadia spoke, she startled both the man and herself just a little.

She said, "Hey, listen, I'm not interested. Get out of my room."

"You certainly seemed interested when I had my hands all over your body this evening."

"I wasn't. Leave this room, now!

"You didn't have this accent earlier. What the hell is going on? He turned on the light, and there she was, fully clothed with a butter knife in hand, "Get out of this room right now, you fucking Nazi!"

He grabbed his clothes, "There's something not quite right about you. Are you a Kike, a Jew? Wait 'till I tell the guys, they will take care of you," he nodded toward Eve's room, "And your friend too." He reached behind him, never taking his eyes off her, and opened the door. She heard him running down the hall.

Nadia left the room, still holding her knife and banging on Eve's locked door, "Wake up, wake up! We have to get out of here, now!" Eve was a light sleeper and was quick to rise, she grabbed her things, and the two ran for the car.

That's when all hell broke loose. Fortunately for them, the key fob had an unlock button, so they had just enough time to retrieve their guns and get into a defensive position. Eve got in the SUV on the driver's side, and Nadia stood outside with the vehicle between her and the men. After shooting off a few rounds so the men would take cover, she hopped in the back seat, slid over to the other side, and opened the window, firing off a few more rounds. Men dropped. Whether they were dead or not, she didn't know or care.

The Aryan Nation men, most of them still half-asleep, were carelessly running toward the vehicle until the shooting started, then they dove behind anything they could, yelling 'Kike', 'Kike lover.' Their shouts included some anatomically impossible obscene threats. One was waving something over his head, shouting, "We know where you live!" As their car sped down the road, the men continued to fire on them until they were out of range.

The women were on high alert. They scanned the road behind them for signs that they were being followed. They expected at any minute vehicles to come up behind them, with weapons firing. Every few seconds Eve inspected the landscape, each time feeling only slightly disappointed that it had barely changed since the last glance.

"What happened back there?"

"The guy," Nadia was still catching her breath, "The guy that patted me down showed up in my room, and I dropped my American accent. He was able to figure out I was Jewish quickly. I don't know how because he's a freaking dullard, but you know those haters. He knew right away that I was Israeli and threatened to get all the guys and attack the both of us, so I got you, and here we are." She paused and said almost inaudibly, "There's just one small problem."

"Oh yeah, what's that?"

"I left my wallet, and that includes my driver's license and address, your dad's address."

"Bloody Hell! Eve's heart sank. She was instantly angry and scared for her small community. "That's what they were shouting. We have to call him."

"It's the middle of the night. Shouldn't we let John sleep for a few hours?"

"No. I think you better wake him up now. He'll have to get the village ready for visitors."

They stopped to retrieve Eve's credentials in the vent at the *Laurelwood Inn* and headed north one hundred miles to the *Greater Rochester International Airport*, located in the middle of a state park.

"Returning the rental car is going to be tricky, Eve. I'm sure at least one or two bullets hit it."

"Maybe if we return it while it's still dark, the rental company will not notice."

When they dropped the car off, the sun was barely up, and they were counting on a less than alert staff. The young man doing the inspection was too busy looking at the two beauties and not at the car, so the bullet holes went unnoticed.

"Nadia, did you learn those skills in your rescue training? You certainly know how to use them."

Nadia played innocent, "I have no idea what you're talking about."

"You know the whole 'I'm sexy, and you want me' business. I'm not judging. I just don't know how to do it as well as you do."

"I will tell you what, Eve, when this is over, I will teach you all about the art of being sensual, now is not the time." Nadia glanced over at her, "You're pouting?"

"No, just bored, and it's a long drive to the airport."

"If I stop for coffee and food, will you stop asking me so many questions? I have no idea what has gotten into you lately."

"Yes, if the coffee and food are exceptional, I'll not ask you a single question until we're back in New Mexico."

"Good, we need gas anyway. Will *McDonalds* do?

There's one attached to the gas station over there."

"Well, okay. *McDonalds* will do. They have passable coffee now, and everyone likes their fries."

"Not everyone."

And this was the banter that continued all way to the airport. Their plane seats were separated by several aisles, so Nadia had some peace.

Chapter Fifteen

The Left Meets the Right

Eve and Nadia made it back to Tres Piedras later that evening. They were both looking worse for wear with dark circles under their eyes and exhaustion on their faces. As they were driving through the village, they noticed several vehicles at the community center and rightfully assumed John was at the center of whatever was happening. Rather than continue to the house, they stopped and explored. John was there, as were all the village residents and Eve's children. There was a sense of excitement and a lot of chatter as strategies were discussed. One would have thought they were planning a festival or a parade, not preparing themselves for a white supremacist attack.

The residents of Tres Piedras could not be any more opposite than their Aryan Nation counterparts. Founded by John and his friends as a community of socialists, they held the philosophy that all people were equal and that spending time helping your neighbor was nobler than caring about one's self. Nothing mattered more to the villagers than their neighbors and their civil rights. The people were not strangers to turmoil, especially against people opposed to their way of life. They were a village of ex-hippies from the 1960s and 1970s, and their offspring were raised with the same ideology as their parents.

When they walked into the community center, all eyes were on them. Eve's face was still bruised and swollen, and her walk was missing its usual confident pace, a tell of hers that let everyone know she was law enforcement. Their neighbors were full of questions, and more than once, John had to ask them to give his two girls some space. Before long, plastic chairs were placed on the stage for Nadia, Eve, with Franklin in her arms, and John, who, for once, without a child or dog hanging on him. That didn't last long; Harper wanted her Papa and fought with Mari until she released her hand. In seconds flat, she was on his lap and ready for the business at hand. They were ready to tell the community the pertinent details about this potential attack by the Aryan Nation.

Eve was the first to speak, telling her friends and neighbors about her undercover mission with the FBI and how something related was impacting her now.

She shared with them how someone unknown to her was stalking and killing attendees at the ill-fated IDEC conference as well as people close to Eve. She warned them that there had been two deaths and two near-deaths, including her own kidnapping and torture, and all of this in the past two weeks.

Lastly, she told them about the trip she and Nadia had made to the Aryan Nation farm and how one of them tried to take advantage of Nadia. Eve described her bravery and how she defended herself with a knife, leaving out that the weapon was a butter knife. Eve went on to say that in the confusion of their escape, Nadia had left behind her wallet with her driver's license. She let it sink in for a minute, then pointed out that the license revealed her home address and that there was a very real possibility that the Aryan Nation would retaliate by showing up in Tres Piedras to seek revenge on Eve's family.

The first question was not 'well, if they're after your family, why are we here?' Because no one in Tres Piedras felt that way. Instead, they asked 'how long would it take them to get to Tres Piedras?' John chimed in at that point and estimated their arrival in as little as four hours. If they had left at the same time as Eve and Nadia, then that would put their arrival time at no earlier than 10 p.m. this evening.

The time was 6 p.m., so the village had little time to round up all the children and older people and ferry them to John's bunker. Teams were tasked to bundle together sleeping materials, popcorn, sodas, movies, diaper bags, whatever it would take so that the young ones would be the least affected and to provide a party-like atmosphere in the bunker. The villagers, not able to defend the village, would take on the role of temporary guardians of the children. In Tres Piedras, everyone was of value. That value just differed based on their skills.

Several of the villagers had survived Vietnam or had some military training. A few were members of the Black Panthers. They were anxious to get the party started. Weapons were gathered, decoys were created, and sentries were posted, so as soon as a vehicle showed up in Tres Piedras, everyone would know.

Eve had expected that this would be the reaction of the village, but for Nadia, this was something so overwhelming and so beautiful she was nearly brought to tears. She had never seen this kind of love in her life.

A plan was finalized, and the villagers dispersed, preparing to do what they had to do to be ready for the intruders. The most skilled of the villagers were stationed at the community center. This was where they believed the Aryan Nation men would attack first.

As predicted, at nearly 4 A.M. when the first vehicles could be heard approaching Tres Piedras. Texts were sent, phone calls were made, and there wasn't a single unarmed person above ground. Sharlo, her parents, Ben Messer, Steven and Zafer, the two guys that ran the construction company, and Jacob D., the *Chili Hut* owner, were all at the community center under the guise of playing cards and drinking alcohol.

Unfortunately, that was the only part of their plan that worked as intended. The Aryan Nation had ten or more members with them, and only five showed up at the center. The remaining spread out through the town and local farms and took hostage to anyone they could find, including Ben's wife.

There was another stranger that showed up at the same time. That stranger received a warm welcome because he had been invited by Eve. The name of that stranger was Jackson. As an African-American growing up in a poor town north of New York City, Jackson was all too familiar with hate. His daily reality as a child and young man had been living in a community where 60% of the adults were unemployed and an equal amount addicted to drugs, alcohol, or both.

Eve had received a text from him a few hours earlier saying he was on his way and he was ready to help her track down Payton's killer. He also said that the business between them would have to wait until the killer was found and taken care of. Eve agreed and told him about their trip to the Aryan Nation farm. She shared with Jackson an alternate route into Tres Piedras, so he was able to arrive in safety and secrecy.

The first thing she did when she saw Jackson refrained from giving him a hug, which is what she really wanted to do. Instead, she loaded him up with weapons and ammunition.

The community center had both front and back doors. When you walk through the front door, you must walk down a long hall. Ten feet down that hall on the right was a door opening up to a gymnasium. On the opposite side, there were two rooms equal in size. The end of the hall opened up into the kitchen, a storage pantry, and a bathroom accessible from both the hall and kitchen. The kitchen had both a back door and counter windows with western-style doors so food could be served when the doors were open and were unaccessible when the doors were closed. The layout was simple, with no place to hide, which could be helpful to the villagers.

As soon as the signal was given, Ben, Zafer, and Jacob were in the kitchen with the doors open and weapons pointed. Ben and Zafer were watching the gym while Jacob had his eye on the side door. All three were armed. Steven, Sharlo, and her parents were at one of four game tables playing cards. The tables had tablecloths on them that dropped to the floor. This was intentional to hide a stash of weapons under each.

When the five Aryan Nation guys walked in, they did so through the front door and went down the hall to the gym. The scene they walked into appeared innocent. Sharlo was laughing, her mother was shuffling the cards, and the others were just sitting back looking at their cards, with a beer in their hands or bottles within reach. The leader of the intruders pulled out a gun and told the gamers to put their hands up. They had no idea there were others in the kitchen, weapons trained on them, just in case the card players needed help. They didn't.

The group at the game table dropped their cards and raised their hands. Three were holding empty bottles. Just a nod at the bottle and a gesture toward one of the five made it clear to each what to do. It happened fast. Sharlo asked if she could go to the bathroom. The leader told her to sit back down. She started to sit, but instead grabbed two of the bottles and flung them with astonishing precision at the leader and the man on his right.

At the same time, Steven and Sharlo's parents took the bottles in their hands and hit the remaining three Aryan Nation guys. All five men were stunned by the sudden unexpected attack and had fallen to the ground but were recovering fast. Not fast enough to take control.

Sharlo was able to relieve the Aryan Nation thug closest to her of his gun by kicking it away and then applying a second kick to the leader's head. Her kick had so much force it turned his body over. When he managed to get to his feet, he pulled out a knife.

He ran at Sharlo, but before he could get close, she retreated to the left, maintaining a safe distance from the knife as her opponent stumbled forward. Sharlo then shuffled up into his space and jammed the man's knife arm at the elbow. She turned her hips and executed an Aikido wrist throw (kotogaeshi), which sent him air-born. He landed hard on the floor. With another kick, she turned his body, then pinned his arm, locked his wrist, and took away his knife.

Before he could attempt to get up, Ben was next to him, pointing his gun down and suggesting to the leader not to move. He then looked over at Sharlo and complimented her, "You moved so fast I couldn't follow. I really need to take your class."

Sharlo laughed, "About time. How long have I been trying to get you in to train, five or more years?" Ben and Sharlo grew up together and often acted more like brother and sister than friends. They looked over at the other four guys, all on the floor and in a surrender pose.

"Hey, mom, do you think the guy knows a sixty-year-old woman just kicked his ass? What moves did you do?"

Sharlo was proud of her mother.

"I'm sure he'll think twice before threatening an older person, that is if we let him live," she winked at Sharlo. "I did a redirect, spinning under his arm and used a Sankyo wrist lock. Then another spin to take away his knife and did a follow up with a strike to the solar plexus using the butt end of his knife," She grinned, "To finish, I applied pressure to his elbow with the knife handle and pinned him face down on the floor."

"Impressive, mom. I don't think I've seen you make that move before. I bet I can guess how dad got his guy: he scraped his wrist bone down his opponent's arm and pulled to get him off-balance, then he likely reversed direction while controlling his elbow and applied an Ikkyo wrist lock, stepped forward into an elbow lock. And ta-da...disarmed."

"That's right, how'd you know?" Her father inquired.

"I saw him attack you with a horizontal slash from right to left, aiming near your stomach. What else would you do?" Sharlo grinned. This was her first real fight, and she was ready for more.

"Hey guys, Ben and I are going to go check on people. It looks like you have this taken care of."

Steven, Zafer, and Jacob each had their weapons pointed at the Aryan Nation guys. They looked crestfallen over the idea that they would have to stay there and babysit the captives with Sharlo's parents."

Sharlo's mom saw the look as well, and with duct tape in one hand and zip ties in another, she said, "You guys go. Your dad and I have this. Have fun!"

The five of them took off, heading to the home closest to the community center. It belonged to Mrs. Beckman. Sharlo knocked on the door using the Tres Piedras knock, three short, three long, one short. No one answered the door, but they heard noises inside. The door was unlocked. They opened it and looked around. Mrs. Beckman was lying on the floor with a gash on her neck, and they could hear people upstairs. Zafer yanked off his backpack and pulled out a first aid kit. He would put his EMT training to good use. Ben and Sharlo headed upstairs. Ben whispered to Sharlo, "I get to go first this time!" She nodded in agreement.

As Ben strolled down the hall, he grabbed a candle stick off a hall table. He knew Rule #1, anything and everything can be a weapon. You just need a working brain to figure out how to make it useful. He spotted a punk poking through Mrs. Beckman's jewelry box, shoving items into his pocket. Ben stage whispered a "Hey, you!" And when the man turned around, he simultaneously threw the candle at him and ran in the same direction, a one-two win. First, the candle on the head. Then, when the Aryan Nation man lifted his hand to try to prevent the candle from hitting him, Ben executed a lateral kick to his knee, disabling him.

He heard a noise behind him and turned around. There was Sharlo, grinning and practically jumping up and down, "Well done, my friend, next?"

"My house is next door, but my wife should be with my children and the Hutaree women on the farms that John, Eve, and Nadia are searching. I do see the light on. Let's just go verify and make sure no one is robbing us.

Zafer stayed with Mrs. B.; Steven and Jacob left to check on the homes on Rodeo Road; Ben and Sharlo headed over by the lumberyard.

Nadia, Eve, and Jackson were checking county road B124. The farm they first came to was the designated safe house. Mari and other Tres Piedras women were waiting. As soon as they walked in, they knew something was wrong. Eve heard a woman crying. She and Mari headed upstairs toward the sound while Jackson checked out the lower floor. The first door had on it a homemade sign with the name Olivia spelled in the crooked crayon font of someone first learning to write.

Nadia did not hesitate; she opened the door. There before her was the Aryan Nation man that had presented himself to Nadia that night on the farm. He had Ben's wife, Sophia, strapped down to a small twin bed with a Barbie comforter half on the bed, and half on the floor, her blouse was torn open, and her jeans and panties pulled down. The man was at the edge of the bed, kneeling over her, unzipping his pants, when Nadia walked up to him, pulled his head back, and slit his neck from ear to ear. Blood poured out, and much of it landed on Sophia. Her body started shaking, and she tried to free her arms and legs. Out of her mouth came a scream so loud that Eve feared other Aryan men would show up. Eve quickly went to her side and whispered to her, it's me, John's daughter, Ben's friend, Shhhh...." Her body relaxed, but she never let her eyes leave Eve's.

Nadia shoved the body onto the floor and tossed her knife to Eve, who caught it and cut the zip ties that bound the woman. When that was done, Nadia joined Jackson downstairs and left Eve to comfort the woman.

Eve did just that. She helped the woman into the shower and turned on the water. Eve started to go find clothes, but Sophia asked her to stay. Once she was clean of the blood, she wrapped up in a towel and went into the next bedroom, where they found some yoga pants and a tee.

When the two made it downstairs, they found three ladies on the sofa and one in the kitchen with the kettle on. Another had her head in the refrigerator. Jackson and Nadia were nowhere to be seen. When the ladies got a look at Sophia, they all started talking at once. Eve asked them to tell her what had happened.

"Two men came into the farm. One used the front door, the other the back. They had guns and made all the ladies go into the living room. The one upstairs kept watching Sophia, and after saying something to the other man, he dragged her upstairs. That happened only five or so minutes before you three came in. The other guy ran out the back as soon as he heard you at the front door. You girls went upstairs, and your handsome African American friend chased down the other one. When John's girlfriend, what a lovely lady, a bit young maybe, but I don't judge, anyway, when she asked, we told her they went out the back door, and she followed. She sure looks tough, though. I don't think she has anything to worry about..." the voice prattled on, but Eve stopped listening.

Eve went out the back door and came upon Jackson, Nadia, and a dead man on the ground. She looked up at the two and raised her eyebrows...

"What?" Nadia said, "It wasn't me," but then, in a voice barely a whisper, she added, "This time."

"I did it, and the asshole deserved it, he shot at me. He missed, of course. The man had no idea how to shoot a gun, probably thought it just looked cool owning one and pulling it out at convenient times."

"That makes two dead in this house. We need to call it in." Eve shared with them.

"I'll tell John. He's keeping track of Aryan Nation guys and locations. He has some guys picking up the dead and wounded, leaving them at Doc Marconi's office. I think Zafer, Jacob, and Steven are helping with the wounded. There's nothing we can do about the dead. Nadia pulled out her phone.

A few of the villagers had been injured. The Chili Hut's wife, Bella, was hit upside the head with the butt of a gun and ended up with a concussion she would brag about for years to come. The community center meetings would never be the same.

When everything was all said and done, the five in the center and a few more at the farms were the only Aryan Nation guys still alive and in reasonably good health. Two others had serious injuries, and three were dead. They gathered the intruders who were still breathing into the gymnasium. Two of them huddled together on the floor, crying. They looked quite young and scared. Eve heard some of the other Aryan Nation men making fun of the ones crying, so she went over to them and gave them a good kick, and said with disgust, "You'll find bullies everywhere."

Nadia grabbed a couple bottles of water and granola bars and gave them to the teens. They looked hesitant to take them, so she tossed them on the ground nearby where they could reach them.

Dr. Marconi was here in her long white coat, more for a prop than as a healer.

John stood up in front of the Aryan Nation men and announced, "The battle is over, and you lost. You now have two choices, grab your dead and injured and get the hell out of New Mexico, or stay and have Dr. Marconi," he nodded his head in her direction, and she held up a few syringes, "Inject whatever she has in her syringes, and you'll wake up in the desert too far out to make it back without dying of dehydration or sunstroke."

Their leader, the one Sharlo had bested, said they would leave without trouble. One by one, their bonds were cut, and they were escorted to their vehicles. Their dead were on the ground nearby. Zafer, Steven, and Jacob, all trained medics, had taken care of the wounded as best they could. Now it's up to them to make sure their people lived or died. The Aryan Nation would be getting no more help from the Tres Piedras villagers.

The sun was rising by the time they were driving down the road, and the residents had to get their village back in order. The mood was jovial. Sophia's neighbors talked about how brave she had been. Mrs. Beckman had a horde of former students listening to her tale. The other ladies at the farm decided their next book club selection would definitely have to be a thriller. The challenge would be to find fiction that could compare to the adventures of the residents of Tres Piedras. That would prove difficult, especially after tonight.

They decided to leave the children in the bunker but changed out their guardians. The general conclusion was that the older people needed their own beds, and the young folks would be just fine on bunks built fifty years ago with mattresses nearly as old. Mari and her sister-in-law, Emily, promised to make breakfast for anyone in need promptly at four in the afternoon.

Chapter Sixteen

After the Raid

With just a few hours of sleep, Jackson, Eve, John, and Nadia sat around the kitchen table, working together to examine the facts. Eve begrudgingly shared with Jackson the photos of Payton that she had retrieved from her secure Inbox. The images included Payton and Eve walking down the street, Payton standing alone at a busy intersection, and lastly, Payton prone on the ground, body at angles that clearly indicated he was dead.

Jackson examined the photos with wide eyes and

raised eyebrows, the shock of seeing his best friend dead in photos was too much for him to handle. His face flushed, and the thud from the pounding of his fist on the table startled them all. Eve knew he blamed her but was not prepared for the look he gave her. Had she not been so well trained, she would have missed it. The look was so sudden he was likely unaware he did it, but the look was so venomous, so threatening, that she found herself backing away from him. All the while, Nadia was attempting to offer him comfort. He shied away from her attempts but accepted the cup of coffee John handed him.

Jackson held the cup so tight that the handle cracked. There was a coldness in his eyes and a concentrated glare that was both focused on Eve and straight through her. His posturing was an attempt to mask the tears welling up in his eyes. John took the cup away and suggested he and Jackson take a walk. Jackson stood up and handed the cup with the cracked handle to Eve. He brought his hand up to his chest and, with a strained voice, told her he was sorry.

The impact the photos had on Jackson was obvious to Eve. He had transitioned from shock to rage to pain in a matter of seconds. Her immediate thought was, "We don't have time for this," but she suppressed the urge to say it aloud. Instead, she grabbed her own cup of coffee. They were all on edge. The lack of sleep and busy schedule had her feeling like she was merely spinning her wheels, talking in circles, and not accomplishing anything. She, too, wanted to punch whatever was available. She looked around. The kitchen was messy, making it too hard to think. It would take hours to get

197

the place cleaned up, and she was certainly not going to do anything.

When John and a much calmer Jackson returned from their walk, they were not surprised to see Mari and Emily had taken over the kitchen. They were hungry and ready for breakfast. The house was full of children and their parents, all waiting for breakfast and talking about the excitement from the previous night. Nadia was hanging out with the older girls, Rose and Jada. Eve was nowhere to be found.

John made an educated guess and looked for her out by the cacti. There she was, sitting on a rock, looking very much as she had when she was young. Her hair was down, and loose, shoulders slouched, just staring off into space. He stopped before making it to where she was sitting and just looked at her, his little girl. He regretted the years that passed without speaking to her, sharing his life with her. John was grateful that at least Camilla had been there when Eve needed someone. Eve was not one to admit she needed another human, but his dear Cam had always known.

Despite his lack of communication with his daughter for nearly ten years, John had been aware that Camilla still spoke to Eve. He would often inquire, without admitting he was doing so, about Eve's life and happiness. It had been his damn stubbornness that made him disown her after she joined the FBI. His pride would not let him accept that his daughter chose to work for the very agency that tried so hard to arrest him, the people who had kept them on the run that made his beloved wife leave him and their small daughter.

He purposely made noises as he approached her so she wouldn't be startled. When she looked up and saw her daddy, she smiled. He sat down next to her and wrapped his arm around her. She rested her head on his shoulder. They didn't talk. They just sat there and appreciated the silence and the scenery. When John thought the coast was clear and everyone would be gone, he suggested they head back home.

"I have some news, and I want to share it with all of you." He had hoped that would encourage her to get up, and it did. As they walked back home, she told him how much she missed the desert. He asked if she had any desire to move back to Tres Piedras, and before she could stop herself, she blurted out, "Oh, god, no." He just chuckled and said, "We'll give it a few more years and see what you say then."

John did have some unexpected news. While the others slept he examined the emails Eve had received from the killer and had discovered something huge, something he had missed before. "The emails were being routed through the FBI's Private Virtual Network (PVN)." He waited for his audience to react, but apparently, by the looks on their faces, they had no idea what he was talking about, so he had to say it in plain English. "The Killer is FBI." Now John got the gasp he was expecting. He sat back, folded his arms, and said, "Now what do we do?"

Eve told the group there were only four people affiliated with the FBI that knew about the conference," She glanced over in Jackson's direction, then back at the group and said, "They were the Dream Team, the ones that created the Dr. Nicole Mathers persona, and before them there was Aaron Reacher, the FBI Analyst that became visibly upset when he realized I had no plans to marry him, but that was back when I was training at Quantico.

Jackson was the first to ask, "Where's Aaron now?

Eve admitted she didn't know and that she had not thought about him since they parted.

"What about the Dream Team? What can you tell us about them?" Nadia asked.

"The team was directed by a Mr. Smith. It's not likely we would be able to find him. But the other four are Franklin," another glance at Jackson, "...my husband, Joan, Harry, and Wenjun, AKA Wennie."

John chimed in, "Those four created your background and kept track of all your social media, your travels, everything you did during that time?"

"Yes, that was their job, obviously."

John continued, "Would they have had access to the conversations you had with me during that time?"

Eve's thought about it and then responded, "I thought I was being very careful, but I'm not really a computer geek, am I?"

John shook his head. He knew he should've been more careful; he should've made sure that their conversations about the insurance company happened only on secured lines. "Evie, honey, it's my fault. If anyone hacked into our conversations, I should have been more careful to make sure we were secure, not yours."

Nadia interrupted, "Oh, come on, guys this is not about blame or who said what or did what. It's about finding out who is killing these people and who is tracking Eve. By the way, John, have you had any alert regarding Karl or Judy, Eve's ex-girlfriend from New York?"

With eyebrows lifted, Jackson looked over at Eve, "Judy, your ex?" She just shrugged her shoulders, gave him a half-smile, and turned her attention back to Nadia.

"Eve, you need to get on your computer and find out where the Dream Team is now, and Aaron. I will find out the status of Judy and Karl. Nadia, can you call the hospital and check on Jim? And Jackson, how about you come with me?"

"Sure thing, sir." He was not about to argue with a man the just convinced a village to murder people and then go on like it's just another day. Besides, he admired this older man, and his mother raised him with manners.

Eve had to put investigating on hold so she could have some quality time with Harper and Franklin. She decided to take them for a walk in their strollers, along with Mari, Rose, and Jada. They wanted to be certain the villagers were okay and that everything was soon to be back to normal. Harper missed Sharlo, and Eve needed to verify for herself that her super-nanny was unharmed.

Sharlo was the first to answer when they knocked. She did not have to say a word, she just reached out her arms, and Harper fell into them. She hugged the little girl and asked her what she had been up to since they last saw each other.

"I drew pictures and slept with a lot of people underground." That pretty much summed up the life of the two-year-old.

When they had to leave, Harper refused to go. She had decided she was going to live with her Sharlo, and no one could change her mind. Or so she thought. Eve knew better than to pull her from Sharlo's arms. Instead, she suggested they get some ice cream and come back and see Sharlo another day. After ice cream, and lots of ice cream, they returned home, and the adults reconvened in the kitchen over Mari's homemade cookies and coffee. Eve wondered why she ever left home.

She started the conversation, "Okay, Nadia, what did you find out?"

"Jim was sent back to Iowa City, Iowa, where he will continue to have medical treatment. He wanted to be closer to his family."

"That's some good news," John smiled and continued, "I checked on Karl and Judy, and they both seem to be fine. I called Karl, myself. After Eve's interaction with Judy, I decided to call her under the guise of a Professor interested in collaborating. Her mood was quite cheery, so I'm sure her family is fine as well. Also, good news. It's your turn, Eve. What did you find out?"

"Well, the Dream Team, with Franklin and Mr. Smith the only exception, are still at the New York

Manhattan field office, so I figured I'd take a trip there. Aaron is down in Miami, Florida. I sent him an email asking him to meet. I will let you know when he responds; however, I have an idea. I think the killer is tracking my emails, and I think we should set a trap."

"Tell us more," Jackson suggested.

"We arrange a trip to visit someone, not on the list, but someone to act as bait, so we can trap the killer. We planned the trips for Campbell, Jim, and Payton, but when I met with Judy and Karl, the trips were spontaneous. There were no email correspondence or plane tickets. Those two were not injured or killed, so it seems to me that this guy depends on learning where I will be and who I will be meeting through my electronic trail. We can drop some bread crumbs and let him come to us."

"It sounds like an excellent plan. Who should we use as bait?" Nadia asked.

"It's obvious, me."Jackson looked at Eve. "Plan a visit to see me. Isn't that why you broke me out of jail?"

"I'm not saying it's a bad idea to use you, but you're already here." Eve countered.

"Then pick some place close, like Dallas, Texas, and I will drive there tonight. You do your normal trip planning, tickets, emails; then fly to me."

"If Jackson is willing, Eve, I think we should give it a shot before we try to go after this FBI mystery agent on his own turf."

Chapter Seventeen

Bait

"It's an eleven-hour trip. Are you sure you guys want to drive it?" Eve looked back and forth at Jackson and Nadia. Their bloodshot eyes, creased brows, and hunched shoulders made her think they should be heading to bed, not heading south.

"Don't worry about us, Eve. If we leave now and drive all night, we can take a nap when we get there. Mari packed us a lunch and snacks." Jackson's tone of voice did not encourage discussion. "Now, do I get a kiss goodbye?"

"Fine, but be careful, Jackson." Eve was worried. Each attack had happened after she had made contact, but still...

She watched him get into her father's car and hoped it would not be the last time she saw him. "Dad, can you get me tickets for early tomorrow morning and email the information to me, as per normal? If we are going to do this, we best get started.

Eve decided to watch *The Little Mermaid* with Harper and Franklin. The three snuggled up on the sofa with a soft throw and a big bowl of popcorn, compliments of Mari. As the movie started, Rose and Jada slipped in and took a spot on the floor. Mari made her way into the room with big bowls of ice cream, handing them off to the girls before taking a seat. John was down in the bunker doing god knows what.

Eve rose early the next morning, threw on a sweatshirt, and had her coffee outdoors. She sat there admiring the massive pink granite boulders that were responsible for the name, Tres Piedras, Spanish for Three Rocks, and thought to herself she could move back, maybe when she retired. The FBI has a mandatory retirement age of fifty-seven, so she had several years to go. She wasn't in the mood for the flight and ended up wearing a pair of worn jeans, a clean Wonder Woman vintage graphic tee, and an ill-fitting jacket that belonged to her dad.

When she arrived at the airport, she walked straight to the gate, found a remote spot, and sat there until it was time to board. Her senses had been dulled by the numerous flights over the past weeks. No longer did the smells of hot food from the food courts, the noises of micro conversations, or the rigidity of the gate seats affect her. She still found the people a great annoyance. The long lines were torture with people bumping into one another, and just this morning, an oblivious traveler had run over her foot with a heavy piece of luggage. Eve had been too distracted to even fantasize about strangling them.

They had chosen the *Hotel Anatole* because of its location and size. Its location borders uptown and downtown Dallas. It was a first for Eve to be immersed in art while heading to her room, and when she walked into her Asian-inspired suite with spa-like comforts and grand style, she perked up. One look at the bed, and she knew her stiff neck and shoulders would improve after sleeping there. Her sensory numbness was waning just from being in the space.

The strategy was to meet Jackson at the *Dallas World Aquarium* at two in the afternoon. Their rendezvous would take place on the third floor at T*he Jungle Café*. Nadia would be lurking nearby, with her eyes on everything and everyone. After their time together, Jackson would do his own thing, and he would appear to be alone and exposed.

Eve drove her rental to the Aquarium earlier than planned. She was feeling anxious and wanted to set eyes on Jackson, ensuring he was safe. A glass of iced sweet tea quenched her thirst, but she had no appetite. What she wanted to do was to walk around, maybe pace back and forth, not just sit and wait. She was having trouble focusing. Instead, she found herself sitting there biting her lip, playing with her hair, and rubbing her aching neck.

When Jackson was ten minutes late, she considered the possibility that he had overslept and refused to worry. When he was twenty minutes late, she pondered the likelihood that he was lost, but when Jackson was thirty minutes late, she was not sitting around any longer. As she stood up to track him down, she saw him sauntering in as if it were just another day. As soon as he was close enough, she hit him. She continued to do so until he wrapped his arms around her and held her tight, whispering into her ear how sorry he was.

"Why were you so late?"

"I'm sorry, your dad's car let me down, or rather the size of his gas tank, but I'm here now," He leaned back to look into her eyes, "And starving."

She pulled away and almost threw a menu at him. "Flatbread pizza for me. What about you, Eve?" He chuckled.

"I'm not hungry." Jackson could not believe what he said he was hearing. This woman was always hungry. He decided not to ask if Eve was okay because she had no reason to be okay. Nothing about her life right now was okay.

When their lunch was over, they left the café and found themselves at the top of the rainforest exhibit. They walked arm-in-arm and gave the impression to all around them that they were a happy couple. They observed exotic birds and chose their favorites. Jackson liked the *Cocks-of-the-Rock*, big surprise. Eve preferred the toucans and admitted it had to do with eating Fruit Loops as a child. As they meandered about, they studied everyone around them.

Two floors below in the aquarium, they discovered black-footed and blue penguins. After their visit with the penguins, they started thinking the plan may not work, but it did not stop them from having a good time. When the day trip was over, they gave each other a big hug, and Eve slipped her spare hotel key card into his pocket; then, they departed ways.

Nadia was nearby, watching and videotaping everyone walking in and out of the Aquarium. Nadia was rarely without her weapons. She had a small arsenal in her rental car. This was one of the reasons they had decided to drive down. When she saw Jackson and Eve leave, she watched Eve walk up to her own rental and Jackson get into John's car. She had been watching from across the street the whole time, so she knew their cars had not been tampered with.

She followed Jackson first to the *Star Liquor, Beer & Wine*, and then to his hotel, the *Crowne Plaza Dallas Downtown*. He sat out at the pool drinking all afternoon and then went back up to his hotel room, presumably to sleep through the night. What anyone watching would not know was that the beverages he had purchased and had been drinking were nonalcoholic and that his semi-alcoholic stupor was faked. The show seemed to be all for naught. No one showed up. Nadia and Eve were always nearby, watching, but saw nothing suspicious.

In the early morning, Jackson headed over to the Anatole to join Eve and Nadia. He did a walk-around before heading up to their room. When he walked in, he found them both asleep on each of the two queen beds. Jackson had no choice but to kick off his shoes, pull off his jeans, and curl up next to Eve. She woke when he crawled in and snuggled up next to her. As she relaxed into him, she could not think of a better way to nap. She smiled contentedly and fell into a deep, restful sleep.

When Eve reawakened, Nadia had just finished showering and was packing her weapons. She had ordered a fresh pot of coffee and bagels from room service, and the scent of fresh-brewed coffee pulled Eve away from Jackson, as Nadia had planned.

Eve added a large amount of cream cheese to her bagel. Her appetite had apparently returned. It may have been due to having both Nadia and Jackson safe in front of her. As soon as Jackson woke, they made a conference call with John to fill him in.

"Well, we tried," Jackson informed him, "Eve and I spent a few hours out together, and then the ladies left me alone for the rest of the day and evening, but it didn't seem to work. I did not spot anyone. Eve, have you analyzed the video while I was sunbathing by the pool?"

"We watched the video but did not see anyone suspicious." Eve paused. "This thoroughly destroys my theory. Now it's time to go to them. It looks like I'll be on the first plane out tomorrow to New York and then from New York to Miami if it all works out with Aaron. Hopefully will be closer to figuring this out."

"Eve, I think you need to take Nadia or Jackson."

John sounded worried. "Especially when you're starting to close in on this guy, don't you think one or both should be with you?"

"No, Dad. I don't think they should come with me. I think bringing Jackson to the FBI field office in New York or Miami, Florida, would likely get him looked at too closely by the FBI and maybe land him back in jail. Nadia doesn't have the clearance to go inside with me. She would just have to be somewhere waiting, and then there's a chance that would make her a target, so the answer is no. I think they both should go back to Tres Piedras. There is always a possibility that the Aryan Nation will come back.

Although John did not want to admit it, he believed she was correct. This was something she would have to do on her own. Eve was right. There's always a chance that additional Aryan Nation members could show up. If they do, God helps them. A repeat visit would not be met with mercy.

Eve did not have a return flight to Tres Piedras. She had known she would be driving back with Jackson and Nadia or heading to New York.

Chapter Eighteen

Dream Team Meetup

Time was running out. Eve only had 4 days left of maternity leave. Regardless of the fact that she was incredibly exhausted and recovering from injuries, she was not about to give up. Once again, she hopped on the plane to *La Guardia* and headed straight for the FBI field office on the corner of Broadway and Worth, lower Manhattan.

Although Eve had been assigned to this office for several years, protocol dictates that if you show up at an FBI field office to which you are not currently assigned, you must first meet with the Special Agent in Charge, the SAC. At the time of Eve's departure, the SAC was Special Agent Adam Lange.

She had a great deal of respect for SAC Lange. He was an honorable man who cared about everyone working for him. It would be fair to say he was a father figure to most of the new agents. When she had screwed up, he had let her know it, but in a fatherly way, not in a boss way. Most agents ended up feeling worse because they had disappointed him rather than for the punishment that was bestowed upon them. Eve respected that.

When she entered the building and made it past the first level of security, she noticed a new face on the wall. SAC Lange was now at headquarters and had been replaced with SAC Marissa Reisen. Eve knew nothing about this woman, but she would have to get through her to talk to her dream team.

Eve impatiently waited for her turn to meet SAC Reisen. A persistent young professional, looking as if she were barely out of high school, directed her to sit down. She may be young-looking, but Eve knew the requirements. At that level, an advanced degree and additional training were both necessary. This girl had put in some time to get here. Eve was getting older, so everyone around her looked like they were children.

The young woman offered her a coffee which Eve graciously accepted, black, no sugar, no cream. She relaxed a bit as she sat there enjoying her coffee, then a buzzer sounded, and she was told the SAC was ready to see her.

She walked into the office; an office Eve had been in

several times under the leadership of SAC Adam Lange, which now looked very different.

What was once an office that exuded humility, love and family now said I am a cold calculating bitch and don't mess with me, or as some would call it, a minimalist style. The room looked quite elegant with simplicity and modesty but lacked any personal touch, no photos of children or partners, nothing that could give you a glimpse into the person across the desk. The sofa, desk, and chairs were designed from basic geometric forms, shapes with graceful and elegant colors and textures. There was a hit of traditional Japanese, visible in the accessories, with a neutral palette of whites, beiges, and grays.

Eve stood there until SAC Reisen directed her to sit down. "Special Agent Black, welcome back. I have heard quite a lot about you from my predecessor SAC Lange. It sounds like you kept him on his toes." She laughed, "And I'm sure he deserved every bit of it. He's a terrific guy, and you were very lucky to have someone like him."

Eve nodded, "Yes, ma'am, he is, and I felt honored."

"I am curious, Eve. What has brought you here, not just back to the field office, but to New York City?"

"It's purely personal, ma'am. During a particular undercover case, I got to know the team very well. I was already in New York visiting some college chums, so I decided to stop by and see how Harry, Joan, and Wennie were doing."

"Now, contrary to what you may think, Special Agent Black, positions such as Special Agent in Charge, are not given randomly. She looked through Eve and seemed to be slightly amused. "They're given to agents that excel in the field. I've learned to not trust everything that passes the lips of others and often go with my gut." She looked right at Eve and said, "Quite frankly, I don't believe you. So, unless you want to tell me your real reason for being here, access is denied."

Eve had not been expecting that and did not know how to proceed. There was a long pause in the conversation, with both ladies looking at each other. At one point, SAC Reisen decided enough of her time had been wasted and started to stand. Eve knew she either had to be honest or offer a more plausible story, or she would be shown the door.

Eve put on her very best I'm sharing something deeply personal with you act. "I'm afraid SAC Reisen, you're right. My motivation is not just to say hi to them. The truth is, I married Franklin. Franklin worked with these three people on various jobs before I met him. They know him well. I've been married to Franklin now for three years, and we have two children. I'm starting to worry that there's just something not right. Eve paused. She widened her eyes and bid tears to well up. "Like you, I've learned to trust my gut." Eve was quite the actress. She was warming to the part. She continued, using all the non-verbal's she could think of to corroborate her story. She paced and spoke with emotion, choking on cue. Her voice was a bit shaky, her words coming across as disjointed. She dabbed at her eyes.

"To be honest, ma'am, I think he's cheating on me or something..." she trailed off. "I just don't know... I thought if I talked to them that I'd get to know a little more about Franklin, you understand, from their side, from their experience. Maybe they know something I do not. I'd just feel a lot more comfortable if I had some insight into his behavior. I have just a few days before my maternity leave is up, and I'll be going back there. I'm uncertain what I'm going back to or to whom. "Eve sat back down and put her face in her hands. SAC Reisen said nothing.

Eve heaved a great sigh and threw up her last line, "I wasn't as upfront as this when you first asked me. I just felt my situation too personal and not something I could share with a superior."

Eve was certain that SAC Reisen would know about her marriage to Franklin. She would also likely know that Eve was on maternity leave. By weaving these truths into her story, she would be more easily believed.

SAC Reisen had stood and studied Eve throughout her emotional outburst. She sat back down, leaned forward, put her arms in front of her, and clasped them together on the table. "I'm sorry to hear this, Eve. I did know you were married to Mr. Johnson. He was a well-respected professional while in this office and, to the best of my knowledge, is equally respected at his new office, your office, in Mobile, Alabama. If he is having an affair, that is something that should be brought to the attention of the FBI because morals and integrity are the backbones of this organization. If one of our agents is lacking those traits, well, they can't really be of good service, can they?"

Bloody hell, this woman is good. Eve wasn't a hundred percent sure SAC Reisen was talking about

Franklin. She could not question that right now. She had to push this forward. "Correct, ma'am." She felt saying the least amount of words was best in this scenario, so she wasn't going to embellish her story any further.

SAC Reisen stood up briskly and stated, "Let's go meet your Dream Team. They're not all working on the same mission at the moment, but they should all still be in the office. Please leave your cup with Miss Winslow, my assistant, and follow me."

As they walked down the hall, Eve followed SAC Reisen, sizing her up. She was not a very tall woman, but she walked with her back straight and like she had a purpose, so everyone should get out of her way. Eve was starting to like her.

The elevator dropped five floors and opened to an expansive space, even more technologically advanced than when she had last been there.

They were greeted by Eve's former partner, Assistant Special Agent in Charge, Sean Peck. SAC Reisen shook his hand and then left them unceremoniously. ASAC Peck had not changed a bit. His looks, and his demeanor, took her back to the day she had met Vic, in an FBI interrogation room.

"ASAC, congratulations. You deserved the promotion. Are you getting any field time in?"

"Not as much as I would want, but I have a few cases. Today I'm meeting with the folks down here to have them help me with Colton Smith. Do you remember him? He was leading that cell interested in blowing up a bridge?"

"Sorry, that's not enough information, Sean. There are way too many terror cells out there with interest in blowing up bridges." Eve was already bored with the conversation.

"The details related to his case do not matter. We heard that he entertained all his prison mates by singing and that he had a remarkable voice, and that gave us the idea to recruit him. We needed someone to do some work for us in North Korea. We're investigating the death of some Americans there. Our team is working on turning him into a star. We heard Kim Jong-un was a huge country music fan, so we're sending Mr. Smith to North Korea."

After a few minutes of standing there in total silence, ASAC Peck apologized to Eve and promised it would just be a minute or two more. Finally, when the silence was too much, Eve asked about his family. He was raised in an FBI family. Two sisters also joined the FBI. Special Agent Kristi Peck was in Miami, and his sister Maddy was at Quantico.

When she asked about his brother, he laughed. His brother played baseball for a national team and was the black sheep of the family. "If you're not law enforcement in our family, you barely get any attention. We grew up on pancake fundraisers and late-night police calls. Our father was the local Sheriff, and our mother, a Fire Captain."

The black sheep was right, he hadn't even said the name of the brother, but she knew his sister's name. She told him how she had joined the FBI against her father's wishes, but he got over it, after ten years.

"Wow, that's a long time to hold a grudge. My sister Kristi and I went through Quantico at the same time, Maddy is younger than us, and it took her time to decide what she wanted to do or to come around, as we like to tease her." Another awkward silence ensued then he said, "Hey, did you know you've become a legend around here?"

Eve looked at him quizzically.

Sean laughed, "Well, maybe a legend isn't the correct way to describe what you mean to the new recruits. You are a precautionary tale."

Eve shook her head and responded, "Oh, really, that doesn't sound good."

"Everyone knows about your time undercover at the conference, the way you blended your pseudonym background with your actual background, that blending of fact and fiction. Despite your falling out of character on several occasions, the mission not only succeeded but flourished under your improvisation. We are now taught to incorporate some wiggle room so that special agents like you can think on their feet and come up with the best scenario needed to perform the job. Basically, instead of becoming circus monkeys, they will get a little autonomy."

Eve wasn't quite sure if she should be insulted by his words or complemented. Either way, she decided to thank him. "I will be going to Miami tomorrow. Perhaps I'll see your sister."

At that moment, a man larger than life walked out

of the conference room. He was a moderately rugged looking young man and moved with a self-possessed arrogance straight toward them. The chap wore a cowboy hat and boots, faded blue jeans, and a black button-up cotton shirt, looking like he had just left the ranch to be there. She could only assume this was the infamous Colton Smith.

Sean looked at his watch and said, "Okay, they're ready." As they passed Mr. Smith, he tipped his hat and gave them a very toothy "Howdy." ASAC Peck leaned over and told her, "I'm going undercover as his agent. This should be fun." The two walked past the cubicles straight into the same conference room that she had been in the last time she was here. "I enjoyed seeing you again, Evelyn. If you see my sister, send her my best. I know working with drug dealers can be all-consuming."

Eve scanned the room, making quick assessments. Joan and Harry were sitting very close to each other, and she knew just by observing them that they were a couple, and they even had the aura of long-term familiarity. She was pleased. Wennie had not changed. She was still a cute young-looking computer expert with so much energy inside her. She was tapping her foot and looked as if she had downed several cups of coffee. Eve wanted to know where she could get a cup.

Eve had really enjoyed her time with Joan and Wennie. Their relationship had blossomed like sisters during the short time they worked together. She didn't know why they had lost touch. She sat down with them at the table.

Joan was the first to acknowledge her. She got up and

out of her seat, rushed to Eve, and gave her a tight hug, "It's so good to see you again. How's everything? How's Franklin? I haven't seen pictures of Harper in months, and we heard you just had a baby boy!"

Wow, they were really up to date. Eve had not been in touch with them since she left, so the only possible source of information was Franklin.

Harry gave her a nod and asked her how she was, but did not look particularly interested in having a conversation with her. This did not surprise Eve in the least. Wennie looked as excited as Joan. The first words out of her mouth were, "I have over a million followers." One would have to understand Wennie to know why that was so important. She was a quiet, well-mannered Japanese girl in the real world, but online, she was an Instagram media-savvy star. Eve had hoped some of the bubbliness that came out in her Instagram persona would manifest in the real world, but after seeing her again, she knew there would always be a distinction between the Wennie in front of her, and the online Wennie.

Eve could only assume that their conversation was being recorded because this was, after all, the FBI. She knew the story she had given SAC Reisen had to be the same story she shared with the team. That also meant that there was a chance her visit today would get back to Franklin. He would very likely find out that she had suspicions of his infidelity. So be it.

If she had to explain to Franklin about this trip, she could say she made an unplanned excursion to visit an old college friend that was having a baby or in the

Hospital, or somebody died, she would come up with that later. Now was not the time to worry about it. She just had to test the team.

She opened with, "I know you are all good friends with Franklin." The snort from Harry led Eve to believe he was not. She carried on, "I have noticed some very strange behavior and was just hoping," glancing over at Harry, "As good friends of his, you could help me figure out what's going on."

"Are you asking us to do a background check on him, asking us to check his emails, his texts, or that we spy on him? I'm not quite sure what you're getting at Eve." Harry's tone and facial expression were antagonistic.

"No, Harry, I'm not asking you to do anything of the kind. I needed to know if you have maintained contact with him. Clearly, you guys knew about Harper and knew about the baby., I'm seeking help figuring out what this is. My gut is telling me something's not right."

Joan leaned in and said, "Eve, as far as I know, I'm the only one still talking with Franklin. I've been sharing the news with Wennie and Harry. When Franklin and I talk, all he has to say is how much he adores you and the children. As far as I know, there's absolutely nothing that means more to him in this world than the three of you. I can say without reservation that I do not believe he is cheating on you! In fact, I would say his love leans more towards obsession and probably gets in the way of his work more than any lack of feelings."

Harry rolled his eyes, so Eve was pretty sure he had heard this story several times. Eve did not for one moment believe Franklin was cheating on her, but it actually felt good to hear it.

After speaking to the three of them, Eve was satisfied that they were not involved in the string of recent events. She looked at the clock on the wall and abruptly said she had to leave. As she got up to go, Wennie asked Eve for her cell phone information. "I'll text you a link to my Instagram," she said excitedly. Eva jotted down her number and gave it to Wennie. Before she left, she had to give the obligatory hugs to Joan and Wennie.

Eve decided the trip was not a loss. She had never honestly considered them to be a threat, and she enjoyed seeing the old place. As she walked up to the conference room door, she saw ASAC Peck and Smith were waiting to take her to the elevator and escort her out of the building. While in the elevator, Smith gave her a sly look and broke out into song;

Hey pretty lady, why don't you give me a sign I'd give anything to make you mine o' mine

I'll do your biddin' and be at your beck and call

ASAC Peck raised his hand to stop Smith, and said, "Colton, this is Special Agent Eve Black. Just a fair warning, don't make her mad."

Colton looked her over and winked, "Can I ask her to have a drink with me?"

At that time, the elevator opened, and Eve headed out the door, but before she pushed through the glass doors of the lobby, she glanced over her shoulder and stared directly at Colton, "ASAC Peck is right, proceed with caution, young man." She walked out onto the streets of lower Manhattan.

Eve was feeling a bit parched, so she stopped at her favorite *Starbucks* and soaked in some New York atmosphere. She was enjoying her tall Sumatra and people watching when, who should walk through the door, none other than Jackson himself.

He approached her table, sat down, and just gave her a big grin.

"How did you know where to find me, and what are you doing here?"

Jackson held up his phone, "Your dad gave me this. It has your GPS location on it. With his blessings, I hopped a plane shortly after you left, and I've been waiting." He watched her face. She did not look happy.

"Don't worry, I've been far enough away so I wouldn't be detected or seen as loitering outside the FBI office, but close enough to be able to follow you when you left."

"But why? I thought we all agreed you and Nadia would stay there and keep Tres Piedras safe?" Eve was definitely not happy.

"Well, actually, you agreed, and your father agreed, but I did no such thing. Listen, Eve, there is someone attacking people you spend time with. That puts you too close to the danger, and I don't want anything to happen," he looked her in the eyes and gave her a small smile, "To you. He paused. "Eve, you are important to me."

"Jackson, are you forgetting what I do for a living? I thought we were not going to discuss us until this was over. I'm not even sure if there is an us to discuss."

"You know when your dad asked me to go with him down to the bunker? What he had in mind was not to show me his computers? Or rather, he had additional things which he wanted to discuss, namely you. He wanted me to know about you, Eve Black, and not the person I had met at the conference."

"I'm not following you, Jackson."

"He told me that right before we met, you lost your stepmother and how she meant everything to you. He told me how she died and how you were willing to do whatever needed to be done to honor her. It reminded me of the relationship I had with my mother and how I was willing to go along with that informant for the $250,000. That meant blowing up a synagogue in order to save my mother. Eve, I see it now. We're both willing to go places and do things...extreme things for a person we love more than anyone else in the world. If I was prepared to kill people for my mother, how could I judge you for what you did for yours?"

Eve remembered his story about his mother. She had cancer, and he had no way to help her. Jackson and the New York 4 had been arrested for planting bombs and sent to jail before trial. His mother had died while he was awaiting trial. Yes, he does understand, and I understood him a little better.

"Am I forgiven?"

"I don't think I'm going to let you get off that easy. I'm willing to let you work for my forgiveness." He chuckled in a way that let her know what kind of work he was interested in her doing. Just the idea caused Eve to blush, which made him laugh even more. His laugh was warm and natural, one that made her want his arms around her. She was married, so that wasn't going to happen.

"Your dad told me Aaron's finally reached out to you and agreed to have a meeting. Aaron wants you to meet his wife and family, right?"

"Yes, that's what the email said, and I have no reason to expect differently. Which is why you're really not needed as my bodyguard." And to herself, she muttered, "no matter how much I want you to guard my body."

"I'm sorry, Eve, I didn't hear what you said. Can you repeat it?"

"What I said isn't important, Jackson. I was joking anyway."

"So now you're saying you don't want me to guard your body? I heard you, Eve. I have excellent hearing," Jackson looked around him, "Even in a noisy place like this." The coffee pots were brewing, espresso machines were grinding, and blenders were working overtime to make all the specialty drinks. Conversations at nearby tables kept the volume high.

When she didn't comment, he shared, "You know Eve, I think the only thing holding you back is that ring on your finger. You know what I've noticed?"

"What's that Jackson?"

"I have been around you for a few days now and not once have you talked about your husband, and to the best of my knowledge not once have you called him. I'm beginning to think the relationship you have with him is not as intimate as the one you would like to have with me."

For someone who did not know her, Eve, the person, very well, he certainly knew how to read her. He was right, she had only spoken to Franklin once since she left Alabama. She did not miss him at all. So, what kind of relationship did they have? Eve knew she could never have a relationship with Jackson, a convicted felon. He had been charged with terrorism, and she was an FBI agent. This sounds like a made-for-TV movie.

"You know, Jackson, there's no way a relationship could happen. We come from two different worlds."

"You just confirmed everything I said about your relationship with your husband and that you're contemplating one with me. Let me just tell you, your father could work miracles with those computers of his. He could remove Jackson today and give me an identity."

Eve took a deep breath, released it, took another deep breath, and said, "Jackson, this is a conversation we should have another time. We need to focus on what's ahead, to find out who killed Payton and the others."

"You're right, you're absolutely right. Tell me how the talk went with the Dream Team."

Eve told Jackson about her conversation with the new SAC and how she had to convince them that she had a dysfunctional relationship with Franklin in order to see the team. Jackson snorted, "And you are telling me that was a lie?"

"Well, yes. I'm not worried that he is having an affair,

so yes. What I said to the SAC and to the Dream Team was a lie. And, of course, they confirmed that they believed the rumors to be untrue. According to Joan, who talks to him frequently, something I did not know, he only speaks about his love for me and the children and, in her words, to the point of obsession."

"Do you think Joan is jealous of you, because that would give her a reason to attack all the people you're speaking with?"

"Oh no, Joan is quite visibly in love with Harry and him with her. You need only spend two minutes in the room with them to feel that. In fact, I knew it three years ago, before they were even together."

"It looks like we may hit a dead end, then with your visit to Aaron. What are your thoughts after that?"

"Frankly, Jackson, I'm so tired I can't think beyond this very moment. I need another coffee."

Jackson stood up, "I'll get it for you. What do you drink?"

"Get me a tall Sumatra, please."

She reached in to get her wallet, and he gave her a sideways glance, "I got this."

Jackson returned, handed her the coffee, ever so carefully so he didn't spill, and had a cup of tea for himself. He headed over to the accouterments counter and grabbed a few sugars, opened and poured them into his tea, and returned to Eve, all his focus on her.

She looked down at his tea and said, "You know the great thing about drinking your coffee or tea black? You get your order right away. You don't have to wait in line with the fancy coffee drinkers."

"I don't mind waiting for something I want." Jackson gazed at her.

Eve looked away.

They just sat there for several minutes, enjoying their drinks and occasionally glancing at each other. The aroma of the baked foods was drifting over to their table. Eve knew this was intentional. They are so enticing on display in the transparent glass cabinet, lined up, waiting to be devoured.

Everything about the shop spoke to the senses. On the wall behind them were different kinds of packed coffee beans in white bags. The whole setting allowed customers to be immersed in coffee. The baristas looked fresh, with clean and ironed uniforms, white teeth, and large smiles for the customers.

All of a sudden, Jackson jumped up. His movement startled Eve, and she started to rise with him, while looking around. He put out his hand, "No, sit, Eve, it's nothing. I just wanted to get you something from their baked goods selection."

She sat back down, and within minutes later, he returned with a wooden platter and handed it to her. There was a piece of warm pumpkin bread with a slab of melting yellow butter. "I asked them to warm it up for you."

Eve brought the fresh, warm bread to her nose, inhaling deeply. It smelled rich and sweet. Picking up a knife, she applied copious amounts of thick, creamy yellow butter. She ripped off a chunk, stuffing the piece into her mouth. Homemade, creamy soft, and warm, before she could stop herself, a sigh of contentment escaped her lips.

"Oh, and Eve, I'm traveling with you to Miami. Your dad arranged a ticket for me on the same plane."

She knew he had just played her, but she didn't care. The bread was delicious.

Chapter Nineteen

Quantico Ex

Miami, Florida is a city shaped by immigration, one that takes maximum advantage of its location, with a culture focused on enjoying life. This means one will find great restaurants, beaches, festivals, and cultural events. It's a fun city where work/life balance is of great importance to its people. The weather is ideal. At the coldest times of the year, the temperature falls into the 50s. On the downside, Miami is slowly disappearing into the sea. It could be time to buy some land further inland. It may well become a waterfront property in a few years.

Eve noticed she had a text from Wennie with a link. She ignored it for now and headed out the gate. The plan was for them to drive separately to the hotel. Jackson was sporting sunglasses, tan khakis, a flowered shirt, and a straw hat. He could not resemble a tourist any better. On the other hand, Eve donned her standard FBI attire with the Franco Sarto shoes. They had quickly become her favorite. Black, off-the-rack pants and jacket, with a Brooks Brothers crisp stretch cotton poplin shirt with a point collar. She dressed for the air-conditioned indoor spaces, not the hot sunny outdoor ones. Eve did not even own shorts, and she wouldn't be caught dead in a swimsuit. The difference in attire would go a long way in demonstrating to anyone watching that they were not together.

Jackson headed straight through to the car rental while Eve decided to search for a *Starbucks* to get a cup of coffee. The shop was easy to recognize; she could see the well-known circular sign before she made it to Gate D10. The image of a twin-tailed, crowned mermaid, the logo of *Starbucks*, and if that wasn't enough to let people know who they were, above the opening was a chocolate brown banner bearing the words, "STARBUCKS COFFEE" in its dark shade of green-cyan, distinguishing it from the surrounding shops.

With time to kill, Eve sat down. Nearby there were tables with cups, packaging, and liquid spillage on top of the gleaming metallic surfaces. Litter that spoke to the urgency the patrons were experiencing scattered the floor. The sense of chaos and hurry was accentuated by the bustling of the baristas. Eve sat there, coffee in hand. At the moment of the first sip, everything else disappeared.

The plan, coordinated by Aaron, was for him to get together with Eve in the hotel's lounge for a drink and a quick catch-up. And then, if they were so inclined, he would take her to his house for dinner with the family, something Eve was already dreading. She didn't do other people's families.

The coffee was satisfying. The medium roast blend smelled and tasted fresh. Once she finished with that one, she went back in line to get an iced coffee with a splash of vanilla and two sugars. On her way to the car rental Eve passed the transportation kiosk and noted that her hotel had a shuttle to and from the airport. While habitually, the idea of being encircled by masses of vacationers would have persuaded her to continue walking straight to the rental car building, today, she decided to go for it. Her budget was not unlimited, and if this hunt were to continue much longer, she might run out of funds soon. Eve was quite fortunate that even when she and Franklin got married, they both kept separate accounts and a combined bank account. Franklin would be none the wiser that she had drained what took her ten years to accumulate.

As soon as she sat down in the shuttle, she placed her carry-on in the seat next to her to guarantee that no one would sit in that spot. A 50-something-year-old man stood above, looking down at her and at her bag, with the hopes that she would pick it up and allow him to sit down. He didn't know Eve, did he?. She just ignored him and looked out the window until he moved on. She didn't care if there weren't enough seats. He could sit on somebody's lap.

The shuttle arrived at the hotel after several stops, forty-five minutes later. By then, she knew Jackson would be settled and probably taking a nap. She went up to the counter to check in and asked if they had any messages for her. Sure enough, there was a small, off-white envelope, neatly sealed, with her name on the front. The clerk slid the envelope across the counter, and she caught it before it fluttered off. With great care, she opened it. As she suspected, the note was from Aaron, telling her he was in the lounge waiting for her. Typical Aaron, always one to leave cute notes.

After receiving her room key card, she looked around the lobby until she found a young man wearing a fitted waist-length jacket with a band collar, double-breasted and trimmed with fan piping, and rows of close-set brass buttons. She walked up to him and politely requested he carries her bag up to her room. She held in her hand a crisp twenty-dollar bill. He took her bag, the money, offered up a big smile, and headed toward the elevator.

She went straight to the lounge and looked about but was not able to spot Aaron anywhere. Eve's initial thought was that he had waited and when she did not arrive, he must have left. Then she heard her name and looked up to see a man coming toward her. He was dressed like the guys from Miami Vice in an effortless linen two-button blazer and pants with a cotton coral shirt. He had a dark tan and a bald head. Unfortunately for Aaron, he was not one of those who could pull off the look.

There was nothing about him that resembled the young man who had attempted to propose to her so long ago. She went up to him, they hugged, and he said how pleased he was to see her again. The voice gave it away. That was the voice that she remembered. The last time she had heard it, he was calling her a sociopath, and he was so angry. He had wanted to propose and planned a special moment, but Eve was not receptive. It seemed so long ago to Eve, and so trivial. Hopefully, this exchange will go better. They were in a public place, so she was at least certain that it could not be much worse.

"You're looking quite lovely. I don't think you've aged a day since we last saw each other."

"You're too kind, Aaron, but this is the body of a married woman with two kids. I'm sure I have aged. I appreciate the compliment, nevertheless. And look at you, no hair!" She laughed, "But it looks good on you," she lied.

"Well, you know I keep fit at the gym. I need to keep my wife attracted to me," he chuckled while rubbing his slightly bulging man belly.

"We're not going to be having dinner with the family, I'm afraid. My wife, Kristi, had a bad day at work and asked to cancel. One of our agents died, sacrificing his life to save Kristi during a drug bust. The good news is that she was able to make the arrest and stop an opioid distribution center. She probably saved hundreds of lives, but as you know, the cost of being an agent doesn't always make the rewards worth it."

"Are you talking about Kristi Peck, sister to Sean in the NYC field office?"

"I am!" His face lit up, "Yes, that's the one, the Love of My Life! Sean helped quite a bit in this case. His team hacked the computers, and created an undercover persona for both Kristi and her partner that held up under intense scrutiny. She had to be away from us for the last few months. She just returned last night, after the bust." He looked at his watch, "I cannot stay long. She needs me, and her little sister, Maddy, will be finishing up at Quantico this week. We're all very anxious to find out where she will end up."

"Now, see Aaron, aren't you glad we didn't marry; it sounds like you have a lovely family. I look forward to getting to know them someday."

"Sean kept me posted on you. He knew we were great friends during training and told me about you going through fashion training." Aaron laughed, "Oh, what I would have given to see you trying on dresses and heels. Sean also said you went undercover at an arms conference and caused some trouble. Now, that I would believe! That was all before your husband put in the transfer requests to Alabama for the two of you.

"Well, Aaron, that's where you've got it wrong. Franklin did not put in orders for a transfer. We were sent there because of my bad behavior."

"No, Eve, I saw the paperwork. Franklin is why you moved. It had nothing to do with you."

"I don't understand. This doesn't make sense. After being reprimanded by SAC Lange and told I needed to attend anger management classes, I was transferred to the Mobile, Alabama, field office. By that time, we were married, so he had to go with me. The move was a hardship for him, something I felt personally responsible for. I even let him choose our home, and made other concessions, in order to make up for it. That bastard!"

Why would Franklin do something like that and lie about it? If he lied about that, what else could he have been lying about? Shit, probably his whole life. Eve's mind raced. She suddenly drew to mind the story he told her once, after drinking too many single malts, about the girl he got pregnant back in England. He and his father had launched a smear campaign to make everyone question her morals, and then offered her father money to sign a contract that they would never pursue Franklin for child support. At the time of the telling, Eve had not been particularly interested. It had nothing to do with her.

If he was willing to do something like that, how could she think he would not do more? He was always looking for the easy way out, and maybe there was more to this. She suddenly wanted to tell Aaron that someone associated with the FBI was stalking her, harassing her, and sending her photos of her contacts, dead.

Aaron operated in a very black and white way. She had to figure out how to share with him her predicament without giving him a reason to take the story to his superiors. She had to trust that his feelings for her went deeper than his commitment to the FBI. Eve took a few drinks of her gin and tonic before coming up with a believable story.

"Aaron, I was working undercover and met up with a person from a case I did a few years ago. That person ended up dead the next day. Whoever did it then sent photos to me of the two of us having dinner, and of him dead in his car, and sent them through the FBI PVN. That is just the start. I'm afraid if I alert the FBI, he will also be alerted, and I'll never capture him.

In addition to the death, he also tortured and killed an old classmate of mine, and murdered another of my undercover contacts. I have to go back to work on Monday, and I'm not any closer to solving this than I was a couple weeks ago. Bottom line, all I know is that it is someone affiliated with the FBI."

"Your husband sounds like a jerk. Maybe he's upset the wrong people, and they are getting revenge on him through you and your contacts. Have you spoken to him about what's going on?"

Eve shook her head no, mulling over what Aaron had said. This was a possibility that they had never considered. "Franklin has no idea about anything. He believes I'm in New Mexico with my dad and family."

"Oh, you mended that relationship, then. That's great, Eve."

"Yes, but it took losing Camilla to fix it."

Aaron looked genuinely sorry for her, "I lost my mom a couple years back too, and my dad's not well. Life really sucks sometimes. Speaking of your current problem, I could do some checking on Franklin and see if there are any disgruntled contacts showing up in the system that could be targeting you. I am a top-notch analyst after all."

Eve let him know she would appreciate any help.

They both stood, gave each other a hug, and Aaron left

with the promise that he would investigate Franklin's activities. He would get back to her this evening with any news.

Eve went up to Jackson's room and tapped on his door. They had agreed to radio silence after meeting up at *Starbucks*. This way, if her lines were tapped, no one would know she was in Miami. All conversations with her father were made via Jackson with the phone her father had given him.

His room smelled of coffee. Jackson handed her a cup, and she sat on the bed, looking out of sorts. Finally, she said aloud, "I'm married to a liar."

Jackson leaned back in his chair, tipping the front two legs up with an impressive balance. He lifted his chin and looked down at her.

"Quit acting so smug, Jackson, I know I'm not the most honest person, but this is different." With a quick kick to his chair, his balance was lost, and he fell backward. The bed stopped the chair mid-fall, preventing him from crashing to the floor. His look of utter shock sent Eve into a laughing fit so human and natural, that her eyes sparkled. Jackson quickly recovered, picked her up, and threw her onto the bed. He straddled her with his knees firmly on the bed and his arms flanking her shoulders. Her laughter suddenly stopped. He leaned in and kissed her. It took Eve back to the night they spent in the hotel years before. She reached her arms around him and pulled him in.

Thirty minutes later, they were back at the table, and Eve remembered the text from Winnie. She opened her phone and scrolled down to the text, and found the link. When she clicked on the link, it did not take her to Wennie's Instagram as she had expected but to an Internet email server, with one email.

My dear friend Eve,

You were always so nice to me when you were here. I should have told you this earlier, but I was afraid. I will tell you now because you need to know what kind of man you married. Before you showed up in the office, I was the target of Franklin's affection, and it wasn't reciprocated. He was relentless, broke into my emails, traced my keystrokes, and stalked me on social media. He once threatened a guy I dated. He didn't know I knew this. The environment was hostile, and I hated going to work, so when you showed up, and he turned his direction and interest your way, I was so relieved I didn't think about what it meant for you until you were married. I should have spoken about this to you, and I told Franklin of my intention to do so. I should not have told him because less than a week later, I found out you were transferred to Alabama. Harry knows, and I told him I wanted to tell you, but he said that it was none of my business. It took me some time, but I have finally made it my business.

Sorry, Wennie

Eve handed her phone over to Jackson so he could read the message. When he finished, he looked up at her and said calmly, but with a world of anger just under the surface, "Could your husband be the one doing all of this?"

"If you had asked me before my meeting with Aaron, I would have said no way. Now I'm not so sure." Eve thought she could read anyone. This was her superpower, one she had been honing since she was a kid. Her uncanny ability to read and manipulate people had made her choose psychology, and had made her join the FBI. To entertain the idea that her husband, the one closest to her, could possibly be doing all of this was beyond comprehension. Could Franklin be a killer? Could he have set her up to be captured and tortured by al-Fuqura? She reached over and picked up Jackson's phone. She had to call her Dad.

John answered on the first ring. "Hello."

"Dad, it's Eve."

"Hi Eve, did everything work out with your Quantico ex? Is Jackson with you? Are you okay? Did you learn anything?"

"Slow down, Dad. Is Nadia with you?"

He got serious, "Yes, she is. Why? Talk to me."

"I think it's Franklin. He's doing this. Can you please make sure the kids are safe? Ask Nadia and Mari to take them someplace. If my hunch is correct, he's going to know I know. He may try to take them from me."

"Sure, Eve, why do you think it's him?"

"He put in for the transfer. He lied about it. Wennie, a friend that worked with him before I showed up, said he used to stalk her, and threatened her boyfriend. I don't know why I missed it, Dad. Now that I think about it, all the signs were there."

"You missed the signs because you were too close to him, blinded by him. He knew how to play you, Evie.

It's not your fault. What's the next step?"

"Aaron is checking on Franklin. He believed the photographer may be someone going after Franklin, using me, but obviously, it wasn't. Isn't. Bloody hell, I don't really know what I'm saying. Let me hang up and see what Aaron finds out. Don't forget; hide the kids."

"Be safe, Evie."

For the longest time, Eve and Jackson sat there in silence. The only break was so she could track down a maid trolley and swipe some more coffee packets. Then she got the text from Aaron,

You mentioned Portland, Seattle, and New York. Did Franklin have a reason to be in those same cities because I just saw some journal vouchers from a few days ago, and he submitted airline tickets to those three cities in the past two weeks?

Eve was dumbfounded. She showed the text to Jackson. His immediate response was, "I'm going to kill him!"

Eve understood his feelings. At the moment, after all, she had been through, she felt the same, but it was not possible. They could not kill the father of her children, or more importantly, could not do it without being the focus of an FBI investigation.

"That's not going to happen, Jackson." "Why the hell not?"

"Because you will be caught, you cannot get away with it."

"Yes, I can." He insisted.

She looked at him with genuine interest, "How?" "I don't quite know yet."

"Think about it, you kill him, they will investigate me, it will come out that I released you with false documents. I know, you are going to say, we'll make it look like an accident, or a suicide. The same thing, they will look into it. He's an Ambassador's son, an employee of the FBI. It can't be done.

"Eve, how can you consider letting him go? Think about what he did to you, to the others?"

"Do you think I haven't? That I'm not completely outraged? It's all I've thought about for the last three weeks; I don't even remember thinking about anything else. You know, Jackson, I've held my baby less than a handful of times since I left Alabama, my newborn baby. I have almost no time with my daughter," her voice dropped considerably, "I was tortured, water-boarded, beaten up by six men," her eyes started to glisten, "You think I don't know what he has done to me, and to them, the others?"

"We can hire someone while making sure we both have two valid and completely separate alibis."

"No, you are not getting it. If he dies, I will be investigated, no options."

"I have it. Create a situation where the FBI or other law enforcement agency kills him for you."

Eve thought about it, thought about it some more. "Are you suggesting I put myself in a situation, as bait, if you will, in my home?"

"I don't want you to risk your life."

"No, no... you are on to something. I will go home and confront Franklin, and if he does something to my children or to me, you call the police, and we both hope he is killed, not arrested."

Eve's flippant response was enough to make Jackson feel the need to raise his voice, "Now you're being ridiculous, Eve." He stood up and grabbed her hand, forcing her to stand up too. Jackson looked down at her, really looked at her. He saw the pain etched on her face, a hunted look in her eyes. He slid her hair away and tucked it behind her ears, and wrapped her up in his arms. Together they sat on the edge of the bed.

Eve melted into the warmth of his body, and that's when the tears started to fall. Jackson did not say a word, he just sat up next to her and rubbed her back, and when tissue was needed, he hopped off the bed, strode to the bathroom, and returned with the box. After using a handful of tissues, she lay down beside him and slept.

Eve woke to Jackson's voice speaking on the phone. She immediately asked him to whom he was speaking. He mumbled a few more words, then hit end, and placed the phone on the table.

"I was speaking to your dad. He said you need to get on a plane and go back to New Mexico."

"Alone?"

"Yes, you are going alone." "And you agreed with him?"

"Yes."

"Why would you agree to do nothing, going on as planned?" She was incredibly confused.

He looked straight into her eyes and said something that surprised them both, "Because some things are more important than revenge, Eve."

Chapter Twenty

One More Time

Eve took the elevator to the lobby and used the desk phone to call Aaron and thank him, as well as brief him on Wennie's text. She also congratulated him on his family and happy life. Aaron let her know that they were there for her and that the next time she was in Miami, they would have dinner.

As she headed out of the lobby, she noticed a couple young things sitting and talking, with drinks in their hands and beachwear on their bodies. She casually reached down and picked up one of their cell phones and proceeded out of the hotel, ignoring hotel porters, and walked a block away before pulling the phone out of her pocket. The phone had a pattern password. The FBI recently sent their agents a white paper about password patterns, including the top five patterns. She decided to give it a try. Her first was a strike from right to left and down, her second, a far-left top to bottom, then left to right across the bottom. The phone unlocked, and she was in.

Her luck continued. The phone had an active Uber app, complete with a credit card. She arranged for a driver. She notes he was Marcos, license #466CRU would be arriving in five minutes. Eve was melting under the Miami sun and took off her jacket and threw it into her bag.

When the Uber arrived, the driver looked at his phone, then back and Eve, and back on his phone.

"Mr. Simmons, Mr. Anson Simmons?"

Shit! She hadn't considered that the phone would reveal her identity to the Uber driver. She deepened her voice and said, "Transgender."

The driver just shrugged his shoulders and said, "Alrighty, get in, sir, I mean, uh, ma'am. Are you visiting our beautiful city that is Miami?"

"No, I live here." She hoped the Uber app did not disclose that kind of information to the driver, and her supposed familiarity with the city would shut the man up. She was in a horrible mood, and chatting with a stranger was not going to help.

"Hello, Ms. Simmons. I am Marcos, your driver.

How can I make your drive to the airport most excellent today?"

"Just drive, Marcos. Everything is fine."

"Oh no, ma'am, fine is not enough. I'm going for perfection. Can I get you some water? In the middle of traffic, he took his eyes off the road and rummaged around in the back seat, "I have sparkling spring...."

"No water, no talking, just drive me to the airport."

"What about music? Would you like to listen to music?" He pushed a few buttons on the stereo, and the car was inundated with rap music, very loud rap music. He started dancing in his seat and singing along with the song.

"Bloody Hell," Eve pulled out her Glock and pointed it at the driver, "Just shut your mouth and drive me to the damn airport."

Marcos looked at the gun and at Eve and just shrugged his shoulders again. "Sure thing, whatever you need." He turned his eyes toward the road, and stepped on the gas.

They made it to the airport in one piece, and as she stepped out of the car, Marcos reminded her to rate him on the Uber app. Eve figured, after acting so calm when a woman, a transgender one at that- pulled a gun on him, he deserved a five-star rating. She agreed, grabbed her bag, and walked toward the gate. After rating him, she tossed the phone in the trash and headed straight to the kiosk to check in with her weapon and carry-on bag.

When she arrived in Taos, she found her favorite

Jeep was unavailable, so she had to rent a Fiat. Could the day get any worse? Apparently, yes. The Fiat's air conditioning was not working.

Her father's home was an oasis in a desert. She walked inside and noticed the environment was void of human chatter. The only sounds were that of cellist Yo-Yo Ma playing at a barely audible volume. She walked into the kitchen and found a fresh pot of coffee and, almost nearly as tempting, flan, a creamy custard dessert, at one time a staple in the home when her Camilla was alive. Eve grabbed a cup of coffee and though tempted to get a piece of the flan, decided against it. Her priority was the family. She had to find where everyone was hiding.

That was when her dad came in through the door and welcomed her home. "Hi, Evie, I'm here to pick you up and take you to the community center for a last-night feast. It's a pig roast goodbye party."

Her shoulders slumped, and she felt even more tired. "Oh, Dad, I don't want to be around people right now. Can I just sit this one out?"

"I'm afraid not. This is for you. We don't have to stay long."

When they arrived at the Tres Piedras Community Center, Eve was surprised to see Jackson speaking with Nadia. Even more surprising, Vic was there as well. Her spirits picked up, and she sauntered over, stopping only to take Franklin from Mari's arms and landing a peck on her cheek without missing a beat.

"I can't believe you're both here," she gave Vic a big

hug, and Jackson an even tighter one. He draped his arm around her waist, and she leaned over and gave Nadia a two-sided air kiss.

The music was playing, and the Center was filled with the aromas of roasted meat and cornbread. Merriment was all around, but Eve was unable to celebrate with them. This was their last night at Tres Piedras and her twelve weeks of maternity leave were over. When it started, she felt it could not get over quickly enough, and now she wished she had more time.

"What do you mean, act like I don't know anything? Are you out of your mind?" Eve could not believe she was talking to her dad like this, but seriously, what the hell was he thinking?

"Eve, hear me out. We all agree that he cannot die, at this time, without you being investigated, and given all of your recent activity, you wouldn't hold up under that kind of inspection."

Eve turned to Jackson, "Why are you agreeing to this?"

"Eve, I told you why. But I have decided to stay here in Tres Piedras, so you will see me again."

Eve was overwhelmed by what they were asking. She knew they were right. She would have to go back to Alabama and pretend to be oblivious to the fact that she was married to a murderer."I don't know if I can pull this off, you guys all know I'm prone to dropping cover."

Vic stepped in, "Eve, I will be keeping an eye on you, you'll be safe, and in the meantime, your new Dream Team, John, Nadia, Mari, and Jackson, will continue to work on a plan."

Eve made her way through the community center crowd and to the kitchen, and begged for a cup of coffee, but only as long as it wasn't more than an hour old, or Folgers. She was in luck; they owned a *Keurig* and were able to track down a few K-cups.

Every time Eve looked at Vic, he and Jackson were in a huddle, talking. She wanted to know what they were saying, what they were planning. Occasionally, Nadia would join them. She would have to interrogate Nadia as soon as they got home.

Rose had taken quite a liking to Harper, telling everyone she was her little cousin, and Harper loved the attention. She tried to copy Rose in everything she did, and Rose let her play on her phone. Eve knew Mari, and Mari's sister-in-law, Emily, but looking around the room, she could not identify any of the other Hutaree women, demonstrating how well they were able to acclimate and blend in.

She noticed Mari spent a lot of time with a nice young man, nearly all evening. She wondered if Mari had a boyfriend. Eve felt a sisterly attachment to the young woman and knew she would have to do a background check on anyone that appeared to have an interest in her. She did not think it likely Mari would get attached, after the abuse she experienced with the Hutaree. It wasn't likely she could trust enough, and to put her daughters at risk again? No, maybe after they went to college.

Ben and Sophia showed up late to the center. They took the opportunity to speak to Eve, telling her thank you once again for rescuing her. Eve reminded Sophia it would be sensible for her to speak with a counselor, but to choose one in town. They had at least two or three. For some reason, counseling and psychology were common professions in crowds like the ones living in Tres Piedras.

The sun was going down, and the sparkling lights made the center take on a magical feel, and that was how Eve was feeling at the moment, magical. She finally knew who the killer was, and she believed she knew his motive.

She looked up and found her father staring at her. He smiled, happy to have caught her eye. He pointed to her watch and mouthed, "Are you ready to go?" She shook her head no. She wanted to just sit there with her coffee and watch everyone. As long as they left her alone, she could enjoy the moment.

Chapter Twenty-One

Going Home

John shuttled Eve and the children to the airport, with Nadia following in the Fiat. Sharlo was not returning with them. They would just have to find a nanny in Alabama. After the Aryan Nation attack, Sharlo wanted to stay in Tres Piedras and help keep the village safe.

Once the three were settled on the plane, Harper started telling her mommy all the fun things she did with her Papa, Aunties Mari and Nadia, and her cousins Jada and Rose. Eve knew that her daughter felt like the Hutaree girls were her real extended family, her blood, and it made Eve happy that her children would have the same kind of family connections she had with the SFH commune members.

Franklin was there to pick them up at the airport. He was happy to have his family back. It had been a rough few weeks, but he had done what he had to do. Eve hated it here. She was unhappy, and that was affecting their marriage, so he had planned a little adventure for her. It had been an opportunity for her to play Sherlock Holmes. He considered it a success even with the unplanned collateral damage.

That Eve had blown up the PCI building on Wall Street did not come as a surprise. He had learned her passwords when they were working together. The woman had no sense of privacy and logged into her emails regardless of who was around. The emails and phone calls to her dad, he knew all about. He was there when she went to the hotel and planted the evidence. He was nearby when she waited for the explosion to happen. Of course, there were minor gaps in information. What she had done once she was in the hotel was unknown, but it didn't matter.

Sending her the photos was a brilliant idea. He had known it would kickstart her. When she told him she was going to her father's house for a vacation, he was not surprised. He thought he was ready. He had no plans to hurt anyone, but when he saw her with that ELF guy, he had lost it. She belonged to him. What the hell was she thinking, laughing, and flirting with that terrorist? It had sent Franklin into a rage. He had wanted to walk in there and punch the man, beat him senseless. However, when he saw the car, the Nissan Leaf, Franklin was reminded of a short brief he had written about car hacking, and he knew he had the perfect method to get rid of the man. Of course, he had to take photos and send them to her. For one, he needed to teach her that flirting was bad, and for another, how else would he get her on the path to solving the case?

Then there was Jim. She used to talk about him, nearly all the time, how perfect he was, how generous. When Franklin found out she was visiting him, he knew Jim had to die. And he would have, had he been wearing different shoes. Eve's resourcefulness in getting the FBI to watch Jim's hospital room was clever. He was quite proud of his wife.

The Jamaat al-Fuqura phone call, telling them that his wife was FBI was risky. Franklin didn't expect her to be tortured too badly. He just wanted to make sure she didn't enjoy the game too much. This kidnapping was his guarantee that she would come home to him. He underestimated her friendships with Nadia and Vic, but boy was he glad they were there; he would have had to step in had they not shown up.

And the Muslim man, he knew she wasn't flirting with him. He just disliked Muslim terrorists.

Franklin was glad to have them back. Eve looked great. A little tired, but she could go to bed early; he'd take care of the kids. He did want to ask why she went to New York two days ago, but because he was not supposed to know this, it would have to come out at another time.

He was all smiles when his baby girl ran up ton

him, and when he bent forwards to kiss his wife, she allowed the closeness, even forced a weak smile. Harper would not let go of his hand, so Eve kept hold of their baby and walked hand-in-hand with Franklin out of the airport to their car and home.

When Franklin kissed her, she recoiled, but was able to cover it up by pretending that baby Franklin had kicked her. She looked down at her son and thought to herself, I'm not calling you Franklin anymore. You are not going to remind me of this man every time I say your name.

"Franklin, I'm thinking we give our baby a nickname. What do you think about calling him Jefferson, or Jeffrey for short?" After seeing the look on his face and knowing he was going to reject, she added in a seductive tone, "This way, when I call out your name, I will not immediately think of our son and lose interest."

"Eve, are you trying to seduce me into agreeing with you? Who has been giving you lessons?"

Eve laughed and squeezed his hand, "Nadia, she has been teaching me a few things about the art of seduction, purely for research."

"Well, if it means more alone time with my wife, Jeffrey it is."

"Hmmm... Nadia was right. It does work."

The rest of the drive back to the house was uneventful. "I notice the nanny was not with you. What happened?"

Really, Eve thought to herself, he noticed. Call me crazy, but what kind of intelligence does it take to notice another human being was not with her? Maybe he was unhappy because he wanted to kill her too? But what she said was, "Apparently, Sharlo was homesick. She didn't want to come back to Alabama. The poor girl missed the desert and her family."

"By the way, Franklin, I made a quick hop to the City earlier in the week, remember my friend Judy? She is married now, with two kids, they had a celebration and asked me at the last minute to go. I wasn't thrilled, but I enjoyed seeing Columbia again."

"That's good to hear. It had been a long time. Did you see anyone else?" He knew the answer; Joan had emailed him.

"Yes, I stopped by the old office and saw the team. I may have alluded to the fact that I thought you were having an affair, she laughed, the SAC asked me why I was there, and I had to think quickly on my feet, so if you hear anything...."

Joan had told him that as well, "That's a bit odd, Eve, but hey, you were never good at thinking on your feet, were you, honey?"

"Apparently not." Or apparently so, because I just did, you psycho.

She just smiled at him, and he smiled back. She reached down and put on some music, so she could stop the small talk and fished out her phone, "I'm going to look up some local daycare centers to get the kids in, but only as a temporary replacement until I can get someone more permanent." Sharlo was already working on that for them. She wanted to make sure she sent them someone that could protect them if Franklin ever lost it.

"That's a good idea," he looked over at her, "Do you want to go out for dinner or eat in?"

"Eat in, I'm really tired, and the kids need to get calmed down." And for the record, she thought to herself, that means too tired for sex. In fact, I will never sleep with you again. You thought it was fun to have me tortured, just wait baby, just wait.

They made it home. Franklin took care of her bags and started dinner, while she gave the children baths, and put them to bed. Harper wasn't happy. She missed everyone back at Tres Piedras, especially Sharlo, and cried herself to sleep.

When she walked into the kitchen and saw Franklin cooking, she let him know how unhappy Harper was, "I may have to make a trip out there again soon." She may have used Harper as the excuse, but it was Jackson she was thinking about.

"Are you ready for dinner? I can make your favorite, haggis, and if you're up to it, we have Guinness!"

She had to smile; this was going to be her hardest undercover mission yet. But what she said was, "Only if you sing our song."

Oh, Danny boy, the pipes, the pipes are calling
From glen to glen, and down the mountain side.
The summer's gone, and all the roses falling,
It's you, it's you must go, and I must bide.

But come ye back when summer's in the meadow,
Or when the valley's hushed and white with snow,
It's I'll be here in sunshine or in shadow,
Oh, Danny boy, oh Danny boy, I love you so!
But when ye come, and all the flowers are dying,
If I am dead, as dead I well may be,
You'll come and find the place where I am lying

OPERATION BRAIN DRAIN:

BACK TO SCHOOL

Chapter One

It Was Dark

Dorm rooms were the worst. When she first arrived at UNM, she picked Alvarado. It was one of the smaller dorms, with only 170 residents. It was the place to be for anyone in the Pre-Health Programs. Cat had been interested in health-related fields, specifically medicine, since junior high, when she lost her little brother to leukemia. When Cat first moved into the dorm, she had a roommate, but now, in her last year as an undergraduate, she had her own place and preferred it. She would be finished the next semester with a degree in organic chemistry and was accepted to Baylor College of Medicine in Houston, Texas, next fall. Her work in Mass Spectrometry under the guidance of Dr. Jorge Alvarez won her many awards. She had three publications and was about to finish her honors project. As a self-starter and a no-nonsense kind of person, she was able to excel, regardless of the obstacles put in front of her.

Her lights were out, and the blinds were closed, so when she woke to strange noises, she had no idea where they were coming from. She was pretty sure there was someone in her room. Cat sat up, pulled the covers up to cover her sports bra, and said aloud, "Who's there?"

When no response came grabbed her phone and powered it up to use as a flashlight. That's when she felt something cover her face, and within seconds she was out. When she came to, Cat could tell she was in the trunk of a car. She had a massive headache, her hands were strapped together behind her back, and she had duct tape on her mouth. She started to panic and thrashed about, kicking the trunk and attempting to scream.

She felt the car pull over and heard two men arguing, "You didn't use enough. She should have been out at least thirty more minutes."

"Well, next time you sneak into a girl's dorm room and knock her out, I will keep watch."

"Fine, I will show you how a real man does it."

Cat had to close her eyes and then open them to barely a squint when the trunk was opened. She saw the outline of two men, both middle-aged and looked Hispanic or Native American. It was hard to tell in the dark.

"What do you want to do? We can't keep driving like this. She's making too much noise. Someone will hear her."

"We need to knock her out again. Do you have any more chloroform?"

"No, that was the last. It's why she's awake. I didn't have enough. Why don't you hit her or something? That should work."

"We can't hit her; she has to show up in good condition, or else we may not get our money."

Cat was hearing all of this, and her first thought was one of relief, she was not going to be raped and killed, or at least not by these two idiots. She decided to play it cool. She calmed herself down and curled up, remaining as quiet as possible, despite the fact that her heart was pounding so loud she was sure they could hear it. She then closed her eyes.

The two men looked at each other, then down at her. "It looks like she's not going to give us no more trouble, so let's leave her be." They closed the trunk, got back into the car, and kept driving.

She was a scientist, and she knew she could think this out logically. What is the most likely scenario? Her captors are human traffickers. She's going to be someone's sex slave. Cat was all about body positivity, and she embraced her larger curves, but she could not believe she was the type of girl they would take. She did not have any boyfriends or girlfriends. She didn't discriminate. She had no reason to suspect stalkers or kidnapping for ransom. She kept coming back around to human trafficking. What does that mean, a lot of sex? Drugs? Would she have to take drugs? Maybe she could pretend she was happy doing the sex thing and they wouldn't feel compelled to drug her; then, after a few weeks, she could sneak away. Yes, that was what she planned to do. So what if she had not had sex yet? She knew she could fake it, she had been lying about being a virgin for ten years, so it should be easy to lie about enjoying sex with strangers.

Deep breath. Cat felt oddly calm; she had a plan. She was going to escape. What would be the first thing she did once she escaped besides calling her parents? Would this mess up her chance to go to medical school at Baylor, or would they see her as courageous and hail her as a student leader? Maybe she would get another scholarship. Medical school would be so expensive, and the lousy scholarship she received from UNM was not enough to cover one year of tuition at Baylor.

---To Be Continued---

Made in the USA
Monee, IL
17 October 2023

44760860R00149